TWISTED

TERRY CAVANAUGH

ISBN: 978-1-965615-86-7

Dedication

I would like to dedicate this book to my darling wife, Ginny Cavanaugh, and to my supportive family.

Acknowledgment

I want to thank my alpha readers, my daughter Teresa Kight, my grandson Wes Kight, and Marcia Fox, for their helpful suggestions for improving this book. I would also like to thank William Pursley, a dear friend, and my professor for his insights. But I take full responsibility for any errors.

Contents

About the Author

My name is Terry Cavanaugh, and I am a semi-retired pastor who has had the privilege of serving several churches in Ohio. Writing has always been a passion of mine, and now, with more time in my schedule, I'm able to fully embrace this love that was born in my soul. It is nurtured daily as I put my thoughts into words—pen to paper, or rather, fingers to keyboard.

Thank you for taking the time to read my novel.

Page Blank Left Intentionally

Chapter 1

It felt strange to be that close to death once again. She was a librarian. They read about murders and mysteries, not take part in them. Maybe "get caught up in" would capture it better.

It started in her apartment.

"Not bad for a day's work, don't you agree, Scruff?" Martha said.

The pungent smell of fresh paint filled her one-bedroom San Antonio apartment. Wiping sweat from her forehead, she sat on the worn sofa, crossing her legs, her long brown hair tied in a ponytail, stuffed into a Cincinnati Reds baseball cap—a gift from her father.

She wore a paint-spattered T-shirt and tattered blue shorts, looking at the freshly painted light blue walls with satisfaction.

Scruff, a rescue dog given to her by her late husband, stretched out on her lap. His actual name was Big Boy, but his curly hair always looked scruffy, so she had nicknamed him Scruff.

She took off the cap and scraped with her thumbnail at a smear of blue paint on the red material. "It sure beats the lime green we've had to tolerate this past year."

She inspected the cap and saw another blue streak. "Wow, Dad would consider damaging Red's memorabilia an unforgivable sin."

She scratched the soft fur on the dog's tummy, and he snuggled closer to her leg and went to sleep.

"A nap is not a bad idea. We've earned one."

She closed her eyes and drifted off.

A thick blanket of fog concealed the ringing she heard. She knew the familiar sound. It was her telephone.

She lifted it to her ear. "Hello?"

"Come home quick!" It was her twin sister, Mary, sobbing on the other end.

"Slow down," Martha said.

"But you don't understand," Mary said. "He is dead!"

"Who is dead? What are you talking about?"

"Martha, Dad is dead!" Mary said, her sniveling slowing.

Her knees gave way. She collapsed onto the sofa, unable to speak. He couldn't be dead. He was so full of life and laughter.

"What do you mean he's dead? I talked to him yesterday on the phone," she said when thinking straight.

"I know, but Mom and I found him on the floor of his office when we came home from Christmas shopping," Mary said.

"Was it a heart attack?"

"No. Martie, someone shot him... Martie, are you there? Are you okay?"

"Shot him? What, who, why? Why would anyone want to shoot Dad?" Martha stammered out as the shock set in.

"Martie," Mary said, "The police are looking into it."

"How could this happen?"

"No one knows. They assume it was a robbery. Some money and clothes are missing. What's important is that you get here as soon as possible. Mom needs you. I need you. You've always been the strong one."

Strong? She was far from that.

"I will catch the first flight out."

She pulled her black American Tourister luggage from the bedroom closet. Her stomach churned. She tried to choke back the waterworks; however, tears flowed down her face and pooled on her T-shirt. Her father and mother had given her the luggage as a graduation present when she earned her master's in library science.

"Your mom and I have a set like it. They'll last you for years. Every time you pack for a trip, know we're praying for you," her dad had said.

He was so proud of her, singing her praises to all his friends. Him dead. It seemed so impossible.

Dad, you never dreamed I'd be using them to pack for your funeral.

She dropped across the bed. Hopelessness overwhelmed her, and she burst into tears again. The darkness of despair rushed in. How could she go on? He was her rock of Gibraltar. Anytime she had a question, he was there. She couldn't face life without him.

No! She would not break down. Her mother and sister needed her, and she was going to be there for them.

Chapter 2

The first flight from San Antonio, Texas, to Columbus, Ohio, was on Delta Airlines at 2:00 a.m. With just a one-hour wait, she had enough time to stop by the Starburst Coffee shop in the airport. She ordered a café latte, letting the aroma of the fresh brew fill her nostrils as she sipped from the steaming cup and waited for her plane.

After checking Scruff's carrier with the attendant, she joined the line to board. She avoided a window seat—too close to the dreary sky she despised.

The flight felt endless. She hated flying, especially at night. The inky blackness outside mirrored her mood: dark, gloomy, and depressed.

Though she closed her eyes, sleep eluded her. Her sister's voice echoed in her mind. She picked up a magazine, flipping through its pages without seeing them.

Upon landing, she headed to the Avis car rental counter. From the limited selection—mostly SUVs—she chose a black Chevy Camaro.

"Would you like the insurance coverage?" the clerk asked.

"Sure, but nothing ever happens in Brownsville," she replied.

She signed the forms and made her way to the parking lot. The icy wind bit at her face, prompting her to pull her thin jacket tightly around her.

"This is not San Antonio, Scruff," she muttered.

The drive to Brownsville would take two hours. A small Ohio town,

Brownsville had been her family's home for the past eighteen years, ever since the bishop appointed her father as pastor of the United Methodist Church there. Of all the places her family had lived—and as a clergy family, there had been many—Brownsville was her favorite. How could something like this happen there?

As she navigated through morning traffic, her father's voice echoed in her mind: *"Drive defensively."* The congestion thinned once she passed the city limits, the white dashed lines of the highway becoming hypnotic. Her thoughts drifted back to her sister's words.

What had she said?

"They found his body on the floor of his study. Someone shot him, but no one knows how or why."

Who would murder a retired preacher? Why? Revenge? Money? An act of passion? The possibilities churned in her mind, making her physically ill.

The piercing siren and flashing red-and-blue lights of a Brownsville police car snapped her out of her daze. She eased the car to the shoulder as the officer approached.

"Morning, ma'am," he greeted her, his nameplate reading

"Henderson."

"Did I do something wrong?" she asked.

"Yes, you were going 45 in a 30-mile-an-hour zone," he replied.

"May I see your license, registration, and proof of insurance?"

He glanced at the documents, his expression softening. "You must be Pastor Thomas's daughter. I'm sorry for your loss. Your dad was a compassionate man."

She gave a silent laugh. Officer Henderson looked like a Ken doll with perfectly combed blond hair. Even in the face of tragedy, her tears mixed with inappropriate humor. She wiped them away, thanked him, and resumed her journey.

Martha arrived at her sister Mary's apartment, a two-bedroom space above a shoe store on Main Street. As she crossed the yard, snow-covered patches of grass peeked through the icy tufts.

Mary opened the door, her neon-red blouse, and matching jeans as vibrant as ever.

"Oh, Martie, it's so good to see you. Mom's a mess," Mary whispered, putting a finger to her lips. "She just fell asleep."

Their mother lay on the sofa in a gray house dress, her face etched with sorrow.

"I came as soon as I could. Have they found out anything?" Martha asked.

"Not a damn thing," Mary replied, fishing a card from her purse. "I'm supposed to meet Detective Daniel Malroy tomorrow at the station. Will you come with me?"

"Of course. Should we bring Mom?"

"Hell no. She couldn't handle it."

Martha winced at her sister's vulgarity but let it slide.

Their mother stirred, and Martha lowered her voice. "I'll get a motel room. What time should we meet in the morning?"

"Make it nine. After the station, we must stop by Green's Funeral

Home. Mom is in no shape to handle that."

Martha left for the Purple Door Inn on the outskirts of town. After checking in, she called for a 6:30 a.m. wake-up call, then climbed into bed with a book she'd picked up at the airport, *The Night Cry* by William David. She barely finished a chapter before sleep claimed her, the book slipping from her hands.

Her slumber was interrupted by the phone. She groggily picked up the receiver, but the line was dead—just the wake-up call.

Reluctantly, she left the warmth of her bed and headed to the gym for a brief jog. Exercise helped clear her mind, and she needed a clear head for the day ahead. Though not as refreshing as jogging outdoors in San Antonio, the treadmill sufficed in the 27-degree weather.

After twenty minutes, she returned to her room, the hot shower stinging her chilled skin and reviving her senses.

She stopped for breakfast at the Dinner Bell restaurant just down the street from the motel. The server arrived, and Martha ordered a fruit plate, black coffee, and a large orange juice. Fifteen minutes later, the food arrived. Martha recognized the server.

"Aren't you Judy Phillips? Didn't we go to school together?"

"Yes, aren't you Martha… Martha Thomas?"

"You remember me?"

"Of course I do. I'm sorry about what happened to your father. The entire town is talking about it. Is there anything I can do?"

"Not really."

"You know, your dad was a great man. He was supposed to perform my wedding next month," she said. "I guess I'll need to find someone else..."

She became embarrassed and frustrated and quickly retreated to the kitchen. Martha didn't blame her—no one knows how to talk about death. It's such a heavy, unsettling topic.

Martha arrived at her sister's home at 8:30 a.m. Mary met her at the door, dressed in bright red baby doll pajamas and a pink housecoat, with her strawberry blond hair sticking out in all directions.

"Aren't you ready yet? We need to be there in 30 minutes." "Don't have a cow. It's been a rough morning. There's fresh coffee in the kitchen."

"No thanks, I just had breakfast at the Dinner Bell."

Mary headed into the bathroom with a cup of coffee in her hand. A few minutes later, Martha heard the shower. She knew they would be late, so she went into the kitchen for coffee.

The television in the kitchen was on, and a commercial for Senator

Rick Phillips was playing. He was running for President of the

United States. Martha couldn't believe a political ad was airing this early—December, and the election wasn't until November of next year. Her attention focused on the screen, and there, in living color, was the face of her server from less than an hour ago. The ad ended with a shot of the Phillips family—Rick, his wife, and their two daughters. Across the picture was a banner that read, "THE

FAMILY-FRIENDLY CANDIDATE." He'd come a long way since

being the mayor of little Brownsville. His rise in the party had been nothing short of historic.

She poured herself a cup of coffee and continued watching the news.

Mary came into the kitchen 20 minutes later, wearing skintight

Levi's, a white blouse halfway unbuttoned, and clearly, no bra. "Mary, are you kidding me? You can't wear something like that to a police station. They'll arrest you for indecent exposure." "If the cop is good-looking, I won't mind," Mary said, laughing.

"Just go put on a bra, or you'll give old man Green a heart attack." Mary returned in five minutes, wearing a brassiere.

"Now that's better," Martha said, stopping her in the middle of the floor and buttoning two buttons on her blouse.

"Prude. No, this is better," Mary said, unbuttoning one button.

"I'm just decent."

"Right," Mary said.

A few minutes later, they were both in the front seat of the rented Camaro, headed for the police station. The police station was on the lower level of the county courthouse. Walking down the corridor, they passed the offices of the county engineer and commissioners before arriving at a large white sign hanging on the wall by a door that read, "Brownsville Police Department."

Inside the door was a large waiting area with multicolored plastic chairs along both walls. A large 4' x 4' Plexiglas sliding window sat at the back wall, behind which sat a female officer.

"May I help you?" she inquired with a sweet southern accent.

"I'm Martha Thomas, and this is my sister Mary. We're here to see Detective Malroy."

"Let me check for y'all."

She disappeared down the hallway and returned a few minutes later, followed by a tall man in his 40s who looked like a police detective from a cheesy 1970s movie. He wore a plaid sports coat, beige dress pants, and a wide, loud plaid tie.

"Detective Malroy," he said gruffly, a cigar hanging from his mouth,

"Can I help you?"

"Yes, I'm Martha Thomas, and this is my twin sister Mary. You said if we came down this morning, you might tell us something about our father's murder." "Follow me," he said.

Malroy led the way down a narrow hallway to a small office. A desk piled high with folders and loose papers sat in the center of the room.

He slid into the chair behind the desk while Martha and Mary sat in the chairs in front of it.

"You must be Reverend Thomas' other daughter. I believe I told your sister, 'I would tell you what I know.' All I know for certain is someone broke into your father's home." "Do you have any idea who?" Martha asked.

"We believe your father surprised a thief, and the scumbag shot him."

"Do you know anything else?" She pressed.

"I'll let you know when we have any other information. We'll catch the creep who did this. You can bank on it," Malroy said.

"What's next?"

"Well, first, we'll see if there are any fingerprints in the house that don't belong to your family or friends."

Martha leaned back in her chair and swallowed hard. She hated it when people talked down to her, treating her like a child.

"Ladies," he said, rounding the desk, grinning, and handing each of them a business card, which Martha dropped into her purse. This interview was over, and he wanted them to know it.

"You'll let us know as soon as you have any other information," Martha said dryly.

"I will let you know about any future developments," he said as they left the room.

They reached the door, and he added, "Oh before you leave, we need your fingerprints for comparison. We'll take them if you both could give us a few minutes. We'll also need hers if your mother could come in later."

He picked up his desk phone and punched a button. A moment later, Officer Henderson appeared in the doorway.

"This is Officer Ken Henderson. He'll take you down the hall and take your prints."

Ken led them to a room down the hall. A computer with a scanner was on the room's far side. He placed their fingers one by one in the scanner, watching as a red light ran across the fingertips. An image appeared on the screen. After Ken finished scanning, Martha promised to bring her mother in later that day.

The sisters drove across town to Green's Funeral Home. Harold Green Sr. owned the funeral home. He had purchased it in 1956 when he moved to Brownsville. Green's Funeral Home still looked exactly like it did in 1956, with the same ugly rose-colored carpet that had only been patched in high-traffic areas, leaving a patchwork of old and new carpet. The same threadbare drapes hung in the parlor.

Everyone in town knew Harold Jr. wanted to update things. Old man

Green always said, "If it's not broken, don't fix it." Their arguments were legendary. Their voices often rose so high they drowned out the ministers during memorial services.

They pulled into the parking lot of Green's Funeral Home a little after 1:00 p.m. Harold Jr. was coming from lunch. He had a McDonald's Coke cup in one hand and a small, grease-stained bag in the other. He looked funny trying to grip both while opening the door with two fingers.

Martha ran up, held it open for him, and then for her sister. The three of them were in the hall when Harold exited his office. Harold Sr. had always made the arrangements—he didn't trust his son with such essential details. Harold Sr. escorted them into his small but meticulously organized office off the lobby.

"It sure is great to see you today. I hope we can get together for a cup of coffee or something before you leave town," Harold Jr.

whispered to Martha.

Once inside the office, old man Green closed the door behind them. "I'm sorry about what happened to your dad," he began. "He was a fine preacher concerned about the church and the community. We here at Green's Funeral Home want you to know we'll do everything possible to make this difficult time easier for you."

She could tell he had used this speech hundreds of times before. It was utterly rote.

"Martha, Mary, have you thought about what kind of service you want for your father?" he asked, and before either of them could answer, he continued, "With your father being such an important person in the community, everything about his service should reflect his standing not only in the church but also in the community at large."

Immediately, he launched into his sales pitch. "We have many wonderful and beautiful caskets you can choose from, but I would suggest our solid oak casket for a man of your father's position and prestige. Yes, it costs more, but your father was worth it. Don't you agree?"

Martha detested the way this old, bald, fat man was trying to manipulate her and her sister's emotions. She refused to look at him and muttered, "Not this time."

A half-hour later, Martha and Mary left Green's with the arrangements made, and there would be no oak casket.

Harold Jr. was busy washing the hearse as they headed for their car. He walked away from the bucket and soapy sponge and cut them off just before they reached the rental car.

"Martha, I really want to meet with you," he said, pressing a business card into her hand.

Martha read the card in the driver's seat: Harold Green Jr., Funeral Director, 120 Main Street, (513) 555-2937. When she turned it over, he had scrawled on the back, "I really need to see you. Please don't call me here."

Martha rolled down the window and told Harold, "I'm staying at the

Purple Door Inn, Room 212. Call me anytime."

Martha and Mary picked up their mother, took her to the Police Station for fingerprinting, and then went for an early dinner. Afterward, they stopped at the grocery store to pick up food. Mary didn't have enough on hand for both her and her mom.

"You will both attend church with me on Sunday, right?" Ruth asked as they drove to Mary's apartment.

Mary looked at Martha and sighed.

Martha cleared her throat. "Yes, Mom, we'll be there."

Martha hadn't been to church for years, but this was for her mom.

After returning to her motel room, Martha noticed her phone's little red message light flashing. She called the desk, and the receptionist told her that a "Harold Green" had left a message: "Please call me at home 555-2334." She dialed Harold's number.

"Harold, this is Martha Thomas."

"Martha, I… I need to talk with you. Can I meet you somewhere?"

"Would you like to meet tonight at six?"

Harold suggested they meet at a small restaurant on the highway five miles from town.

When Martha arrived, it wasn't a restaurant but a dive. She pulled her car into one of the open parking spaces. Harold was already there, so she would have to go in.

They both entered together. The stench of burned beans hung in the air. They walked over the faded tile floor to a back booth. Oh no, was that duct tape on the seats? The server took their order for coffee and left them alone.

After an awkward silence, Harold began, "Martha, I... I wanted to see you so I could explain... I mean, so I could tell you... Oh, Martha, I saw your dad the day he was, you know," he blurted out.

"What do you mean you saw Dad?"

"Your dad was helping me with my problem."

"Harold, what are you talking about?"

He bit his lip and looked away. "I have a minor problem with alcohol."

Everyone in town knew about Harold's problem, but not his father. However, Harold Jr. felt it was a well-hidden secret.

He tapped his heel on the tiled floor. "Your father met with me weekly to help me deal with it. In fact, he helped me get into an A.A group in Columbus. Together, we've been working through the twelve steps."

"I'm glad you're getting your life back together, but what does that have to do with Dad's murder?"

"We met in your father's office the afternoon he was, you know…"

"Murdered, Harold, my father was murdered," Martha said.

"Well, the day your father was murdered, I was in his study. If the police run the fingerprints, mine will come up. They picked me up for a DUI last year, and my prints are in the system."

"Why don't you tell this to the police?"

"I would, but I don't know who to talk to," Harold complained.

"Call and ask for Detective Malroy. He's handling Dad's case," Martha said.

"I promise to call him tomorrow," Harold said.

They finished their coffee, had a piece of pumpkin pie, and said their goodbyes. Martha returned to her motel room and got ready for bed. What a day! The police didn't know who was responsible, and poor Harold was in turmoil. He should just stand up to his father.

Scruff went outside one last time, came in, jumped on the bed, and burrowed under the blanket.

"Time for sleep, right, old boy?"

Chapter 3

It had been years since she had attended church, not since her husband died in a car crash. After the accident, she spent 48 hours in the ICU, waiting and praying. The doctors said he was suffering from brain swelling, and they gave him little chance of recovery. As the hours dragged on, her pain became unbearable. With each passing moment, her anger and hatred for God grew.

Holding her husband in her arms, she swore she would never forgive God, never. From that moment on, she never stepped foot in a church again. But this morning, she would return—because her mother and sister needed her. She would go.

She pulled into the church parking lot. Most of the spaces were filled, as it was just a few minutes before the service started. She sat in her car, listening to the radio as the announcer mentioned that a

Kentucky station was playing "Baby, It's Cold Outside" on a loop, unapologetically ignoring protests.

She watched the last few latecomers hurry down the sidewalk and through the double glass doors.

I hate this.

Summoning her courage, she opened the door of her rental car and walked up the sidewalk to join the rest of the stragglers.

The place had changed. In the foyer, where Brother Lewis had handed out bulletins for years, now stood a welcome center with information about the latest small group Bible studies. Where the picture of Jesus, the Great Shepherd, once hung, there was now a built-in coffee bar with cappuccino machines and Krispy Kreme donuts. Coffee and donuts— you couldn't go wrong with that.

The greeter, a young, handsome man in a blue pullover sweater and beige Dockers, was not old Brother Lewis in his wrinkled blue three-piece suit. He said, "Martha, would you like a copy of today's program?"

She didn't recognize him at first.

"I didn't recognize you without the uniform," she confessed.

"I leave the uniform and gun at home when I come to church," he said, laughing. "Can I help you find a seat? It's about time to begin."

"Yes," she said, "I'd like to sit with my mom and sister if there's room."

They walked up the aisle and found Ruth and Mary about halfway up. Ruth and Mary had kept a chair open for her.

"I'm glad you made it," her mother whispered. "I was afraid you might change your mind."

Martha said, "I almost did, but I'm here now."

She looked around for a hymnal but couldn't find one. Then she noticed movement up front. Three young women and a young man walked to the center of the stage. A couple of older teens picked up a lead guitar and a bass guitar. The room was filled with soft rock music.

Seeing Martha's confusion, Ruth leaned over and whispered, "Our new pastor started this service about six months ago. It's different.

But you know, I think I like it."

Martha looked back toward the stage. A young man in a casual dress took a handheld microphone and said, "Good morning. My name is Chris Butler, and I'm the pastor here at Brownsville UMC. We want to invite you to worship Jesus Christ with us."

When he finished speaking, the music volume increased, and the young woman and young man sang, "Our God is an awesome God..." The words were projected on a screen above their heads.

Things had certainly changed. No hymnals, no organ—just a band.

After a few songs, Pastor Chris returned to center stage and prayed.

Martha refused to bow her head or close her eyes. She had nothing to say to God. As he prayed, she looked around defiantly. Stackable blue chairs had replaced the wooden pews with red velvet padding that she remembered. But as she looked back, she noticed Sister Lewis's face. She was an institution at this church. You could change the foyer, the music, even the pastor, but Sister Lewis was still there, sitting on the third pew up from the back on the aisle side.

She couldn't help but laugh. The church had transformed entirely around her, but Sister Lewis was unchanged.

Sister Lewis was an accomplished gossip. She had sung in the choir for years—not because she enjoyed singing, but because she wanted the coffee break afterward. She and the other ladies would gather around, exchanging all the latest gossip. After prattling about everyone in town, they'd depart with smiles, promising to pray for all the people whose lives they had just dissected.

Martha looked at the program and saw that Brownsville UMC now had two-morning services. The first is a Traditional Service at 9:30 and contemporary Praise and Worship at 11:00 a.m.

It didn't surprise her to see Sister Lewis here. No doubt she had also attended the earlier service. She probably did both just to stay ahead of the gossip curve, to ensure no one else heard the rumors before she did, securing her place as queen of groundless rumors.

The music continued for the next 25 minutes. Pastor Chris walked to center stage, placed his notes on a music stand, and began his sermon. The whole service wrapped up in less than 55 minutes.

Thank God this is over.

But it wasn't over.

As soon as Pastor Chris said the final amen, like magic, the churchgoers surrounded them. How did Sister Lewis haul her bulk from the third row to in front of Martha's mother so quickly? She was the first one in line to talk to Ruth. The way people gathered was like buzzards circling around a carcass on the roadside.

With a sickly-sweet smile, Sister Lewis said, "Ruth, you poor dear. Honey, have the police figured out who did this awful thing to your dear husband?" Before Ruth could respond, Sister Lewis added, "Of course, the choir will be happy to sing at Reverend Thomas's funeral if it will help."

Martha couldn't help but think Sister Lewis was more interested in gathering gossip than showing genuine concern. After she had said her piece, Sister Lewis waddled away—but not far enough to be out of earshot, as she made sure to overhear the conversations of others.

One by one, people passed by, offering the same platitudes: "We're sorry about what happened," and "I hope the police catch the killer." Rick

Phillips, his wife Elizabeth, and daughters Judy and Jacqueline were the last family in line. Rick handed Ruth a box of tissues and said, "I know the police will do all they can to catch the maniac who did this. I want you to know I'll keep in touch with my sources downtown and let you know what I find out."

Was he being kind, or was there more to it? What sources was he talking about? How closely was he watching this? Why was he paying such close attention? Was it a genuine concern for a former pastor?

It was twenty minutes after the service ended before Martha, Ruth, and Mary could leave.

As they headed for the parking lot, Ken ran to catch up with them before Martha reached her car. "It was great to have you in church with us this morning. I hope to see you again soon."

"Oh, thank you," she replied, still feeling unsettled.

She followed Mary to the Beef and Bistro, the new restaurant on the edge of town. Ken's words, "I hope to see you again soon," kept rattling around in her mind. *I hope to see him again, too.*

Martha had lunch with Mary and her mother, and they all discussed the worship service. They purposefully avoided mentioning their father or his upcoming funeral.

After lunch, the sisters dropped their mother off at the apartment for an afternoon nap and then spent the afternoon window shopping at the mall. They visited TJ Maxx and JC Penney. Martha needed a winter jacket—her windbreaker from Texas was no match for

Brownsville's weather. She also bought a white knit sweater and a cashmere jacket.

Mary giggled while holding up the jacket. "A trip to the police station might be necessary. You want to look good if you run into

Ken Henderson."

"Please," Martha said, rolling her eyes.

She dropped her sister off and then stopped at the Dinner Bell for soup and salad. She listened to the servers and busboys chatter back and forth about who had which tables and who the big tippers were. It was nice to just sit there and listen.

No one was asking her about her father, his murder, or the upcoming funeral—just people she didn't know doing their jobs as if nothing else mattered. Judy must not have worked on Sundays. At least she wasn't here this Sunday.

***

She read the headlines of the complimentary copy of the *Brownsville*

Herald from the motel. "Escapee Charged with Pastor's Murder" jumped off the page in inch-high black letters. How dare he? She rummaged through her purse, her pulse quickening. Dumping the contents onto the motel bed, she sifted through the hodgepodge and finally found the business card she was looking for.

She dialed the number, trying to calm herself. *Don't yell.*

"Brownsville Police Department, how may I help you?" a sweet female voice answered.

Trying to control her rage, she said, "May I speak to Detective Malroy?"

"I will be happy to see if he's free. Who, may I ask, is calling?" the receptionist asked.

"This is Martha Thomas, and I need to see him today."

She waited at least five minutes before the receptionist returned.

"I'm sorry, Ms. Thomas, but Detective Malroy is busy. He said he would call you later this morning. Could you give me your number?"

The response did not satisfy her, but she didn't want to take out her fury on an innocent receptionist. She gave her phone number and hung up.

Martha was hungry since she hadn't had breakfast, but she wasn't about to leave her room or phone until she spoke to Malroy. She turned on the television but quickly turned it off. Sitting there, she pounded her fist on the bedside table, watching the digital clock tick off the minutes. With each passing minute, her indignation grew. At a quarter to eleven, the phone finally rang.

She picked up the receiver and cried, "It's about time!"

There was silence on the other end, then her mother's startled voice.

"We just wanted to see if you'd like to join us for lunch."

"I'm sorry, Mom," Martha mumbled. "I was waiting for a call. I'll be happy to meet you and sis for lunch."

"Is the Beef and Bistro good for you?"

"Yes, in half an hour."

She folded the newspaper, stuffed it under her arm, and hurried to the car.

The satisfying all-you-can-eat buffet did nothing to satisfy her anger.

She drove straight to the police station and stormed up to the receptionist.

"I'm Martha Thomas, and I've been waiting all morning for Detective Malroy to return my call. I want to see him right now!" The receptionist turned away, punched a button on her phone, and relayed the message to someone on the other end. After a few seconds, she turned back and said, "I'm sorry, but he's still busy. Could you come back tomorrow?"

"No, I will not come back tomorrow! I want to talk to him today! I'll wait until he's free," Martha almost shouted.

She walked to a green plastic chair against the right wall, with an unobstructed view of the door, and sat down.

She sat there for almost an hour. The door opened, and Detective Malroy and two other officers in uniform walked out.

She jumped to her feet. "I want to talk to you, Detective Malroy!"

"I'm sorry, Madam, but I'm too busy for an appointment today," Malroy responded, turning back to the officers and striding across the waiting area.

She tensed and screamed, "You lied to me!"

Malroy's face turned crimson as he came back to try to quiet her down.

"Calm down. I didn't lie to you—not really."

"What do you call it? You said you'd call me if there was any information about my father's murder. *Any* information. I consider arresting a suspect information. Why didn't you call me? According to this…" She paused just long enough to open the newspaper she was carrying. "You knew about Jamal Richards on Saturday! Saturday! That was three days ago. And you never called. Why?"

"Ms. Thomas, can we take this back to my office?"

"That's what I've been trying to do all day," Martha said.

She followed him through the door on the far wall and into his office. He motioned for her to sit, but she stood before the desk.

"Okay, we're in your office. Why didn't you call my family?"

"Here's what happened. After we ran your prints, we discovered one set in the house that didn't belong. We ran them through our system and found they belonged to Jamal Richards. He escaped from CCI on the same day as your father's murder. They apprehended him about twenty miles from Columbus, wearing your father's clothes and carrying about one hundred dollars of the five hundred he took from your father. We picked him up late Saturday night. I didn't want to ruin your Sunday, so I didn't call you."

"You didn't want to ruin our Sunday by telling us you caught Dad's killer? Don't give me that," Martha said.

"You can look at it your way. I'll look at it mine," Malroy replied.

"Ms. Thomas, I must go. I'm expected in court." He stood and held open his office door, waiting for Martha to leave.

With many of her questions unanswered and a headache forming, Martha headed back to the motel.

She took Scruff for a walk, collapsed across the bed, closed her eyes, and fell asleep immediately. Even though she had slept well, she woke up feeling unrested.

For a late dinner, she went to the Dinner Bell. Judy came to take her order. When Judy returned to the table with the food, she lingered.

"I'm glad they caught Jamal Richards. Now, he'll get what he deserves. He deserves the death penalty," Judy said.

Martha returned to the motel to settle in for the rest of the evening. She opened her book and read. Scruff stretched out beside her, comfortable for the night.

Martha's phone rang. This time, instead of the front desk, it was her mother, Ruth, sobbing.

"Martha, Mr. Green just called. The police said we can go ahead with the funeral." Martha sensed that her mother was weeping because the shock had worn off, and now she had to face her husband's death. "Mr. Green asked if we could meet him at his funeral home this morning to complete arrangements."

Martha agreed to meet Mary and her mother at Green's at 9:00 that morning.

She skipped her workout, which was not something she often did, but this morning, after her blow-up with Malroy the day before and the wake-up call from her mother, she didn't feel like running in place for twenty minutes. No amount of stress or sweat was going to make her feel better.

She took Scruff for a quick walk.

"Hurry, Scruff, I don't have time for you to inspect every blade of grass—just find a spot."

She grabbed breakfast at McDonald's, picked up the newspaper, and drove to Green's. Her mother and sister hadn't arrived yet. On the sports page, halfway down, was a quarter-page ad about Rick Phillips running for President. The ad featured a large family picture of Rick, his wife Judy, and her younger sister, smiling like the all-

American family. The banner read, "Rick Phillips, The Family Friendly Candidate." He wore that fake, sickly politician smile so often associated with Washington. She quickly skimmed through the rest of the paper to

see if there was any more information about her father's murder. To her surprise, only a brief article on the back page repeated the same information from the day before. The news cycle had moved on; she wished she could, too.

She had finished reading the article when her sister and mother pulled in. Together, they walked into Green's Funeral Home.

"Where's your son?" Martha asked.

Harold opened the door to his office. "Oh, today's his day off."

It was agreed that the funeral notice would appear in the paper that day, with the viewing from 2 to 4 p.m. and 7 to 9 p.m. on

Wednesday. The funeral will be at the church Thursday at 11:00 a.m.

Dad's District Superintendent and close family friend, Dr. Joy, would officiate, and Pastor Chris would assist. Of course, the choir would sing during the service.

By the time they left, their mother was shaking. Mary supported her on one side and Martha on the other. They helped her to the car. For the first time, Martha saw her mother as weak and vulnerable. Growing up, she had believed her mother was an unstoppable force of nature—nothing could stand in her way. But now, she was limp and drained as they helped her into the car. Mother was human, after all.

She and Mary helped their mother up the stairs to Mary's apartment. Ruth put on a faded housedress and sat in front of the television. On the screen was a man in overalls, standing in a cornfield, claiming to have seen an alien resembling their uncle Herbert.

Ruth just blankly stared at the screen.

"Do you girls remember when Dad took us camping?" she asked.

There had been only one camping trip for the Thomas family, though Dad had promised to go again. They had loaded their blue Chevy station wagon and headed out for the adventure of a lifetime. Their dad had grown up in the city and knew nothing about camping. Everything he learned about camping came from a book he bought at Borders Books, which he skimmed through because he had been too busy to read carefully.

They arrived at their Big Hoosier State Park campsite a little after 2:00 p.m. They took out the tent, still in the box from the store, and tried to put it together.

The carton boasted, "One person can assemble this tent in fifteen minutes."

Mary, Dad, and Martha set to work, but two hours later, the tent looked like a giant, deflated canvas balloon. Mom passed the time by watching and laughing.

When they were about ready to pack it in and find a motel, the man from a neighboring campsite came over.

"We had a tent just like this one until we bought a new one. Too many kids to cram into that small space," a man from a nearby site said.

In just a few minutes, the man had the tent standing. When they went to bed, they discovered a tent that slept four people and was not big enough for four people and all their stuff. They left their clothes in the car and some food in Styrofoam coolers under the picnic table.

The following day, their food was strewn across three campsites.

"You should bag all your food up at night and hang it from a branch in the tree. The only way to keep it away from those pesky coons," the man advised.

Their dad didn't seal the tent's seams, which seemed a waste of time.

During their second night, it rained both inside and outside the tent. They spent the night trying to sleep in the car—Mom and Dad in the front bench seats of the station wagon and the girls in the back, with the middle seat down. Martha never could get comfortable curled around all their clothes and the leftover food. There was no third night. Wet and tired, Mom and the girls, cranky from lack of sleep, convinced their father the camping trip was over. It was time to find a motel for the rest of the vacation.

As they recalled that miserable camping experience, they laughed—softly at first but harder and longer as the afternoon went on. By 4:00 p.m., they were all cackling. They had an early dinner of lunch meat sandwiches and diet Pepsi.

Martha picked up Scruff and took him for a good, long walk at Brownsville Park. Afterward, she returned to the motel but remembered she had nothing to wear for the viewing or the funeral.

She turned around and drove to the mall. She looked at JC Penney and TJ Maxx but found nothing she liked. Then, walking back toward her car, she saw Slater's Dress Shop. From the front window, she saw they had an excellent selection of black dresses.

She tried on a black strapless dress but felt it was too revealing as she gazed at herself in the full-length mirror.

Next, she tried on another black dress, but it had a plunging open back, which she also felt was inappropriate. She finally settled on a lovely, conservative black drape-neck dress, calf-length with a jacket, for the funeral and a two-piece pantsuit for the viewing, which would pair well with the white top she had just bought.

She stopped at the Dinner Bell for coffee and some strawberry pie. Judy was working. After serving the coffee and pie, Judy lingered and chatted with her. After a few minutes, Judy nervously said,

"Martha, I know you have the viewing and everything tomorrow, and if you don't want to go, I'll understand, but I was wondering if you might like to take in a movie tonight? I get off at six, and a new Tom Cruise movie is showing at the mall."

Martha wanted to say no, but the words that came out were, "Yes, I'd really like that."

"Do you mind if I bring my sister along? I promised her a night at the movies," Judy asked.

"That would be fine," Martha replied.

"Well, the showing is at 7:45. Would you like to meet here at 6:30 before we pick up Jacqueline? We could get a cappuccino before the show," Judy said, giddy with excitement.

"Sure, 6:30 sounds great. It will give me time to change and freshen up," Martha agreed.

A night out wasn't a bad idea after all. She returned to the motel.

"You like this new blouse, Scruff?" she asked, striking a runway pose as he lay serenely on the bed.

Through the cappuccinos, they talked about their school years. Neither of them had dated much.

"Do you remember Billy Davidson?"

"Sure, he was as geeky as I was, always reading a book. What became of him?" Martha asked. "He's an author now."

"Really? What does he write?"

"Mysteries. You might have read one of his. He writes under the name William David," Judy said.

"William David? I just finished one of his novels, *The Corpse Resurfaced.*"

"I don't read his stuff. I tried it once, and I couldn't sleep for a week," Judy replied.

The movie was an adventure-romance, and they both laughed and cried. Judy's sister, Jacqueline, seemed to enjoy the blood and guts scenes more than they did.

The whole evening reminded Martha of going to the movies with her friends from high school.

Back in her room, she said to a tuckered-out Scruff, "It was great to act like a kid tonight. But tomorrow, I have to be a grown-up again." She climbed out of bed.

"Time to get up, Scruff."

Scruff began his morning dance as he waited to go outside. She put the halter and leash on him, and he rushed to the door. After doing what dogs do outside, she said, "Good boy."

She loaded him into the rental car and headed to Mary's house.

She came through the door with Scruff hot on her heels. "Coffee ready?"

"Yeah, help yourself," Mary called from a back bedroom.

Martha made her way to the kitchen, poured a cup of coffee, and opened the refrigerator to see if there was any milk to add.

"No milk, sorry," Mary said, standing in the doorway in a bra and cut-off blue jean shorts.

"Would you and Mom want to go to breakfast? My treat," Martha offered.

"Sure," Ruth said as she entered the kitchen and refilled her coffee mug.

"Give me a minute to get ready," Mary said, retreating into the bathroom.

They loaded into the car and drove to the Dinner Bell.

After they ordered breakfast, Martha asked, "Who is this Jamal?"

"I don't know," Mary answered.

"Bastard!" Ruth blurted out.

Mary and Martha both stared at her in shock. This was the first time they had ever heard their mother use profanity.

"Mom, you never say words like that! What's going on?" Martha asked.

"He is, and he killed your dad!" Ruth said, holding her ground.

They looked up, only to find Judy standing there with their orders.

There was a long silence as she placed the plates in front of them.

"I agree with you," Judy said to Ruth.

"Will there be anything else?"

"No, this will be fine," Martha muttered.

They ate the rest of the meal in a strange, heavy silence.

Martha dropped them off at the house and went to the library.

"You wait right here, Scruff. I have something I want to check out." She felt at home in a library surrounded by books.

Her father always said, "Martha, books are the gateway to knowledge or hours of escape. You create your future by who you know and what you read."

She walked to the computer terminal and typed in the name, "Malroy."

There they were—books by Daniel Malroy. So, he was an author.

"Now, I must take you to the boarder, Scruff."

She took Scruff to Canine Heaven, the groomer and boarder.

"Here's Scruff," she said as she opened the door.

"Just sign him in," the attendant said, turning the sign-in book around and pushing it toward her. She could hear other dogs barking in the back room. The reception area was neat and clean.

"May I see where he'll stay?"

"Sure, follow me."

The attendant led her and Scruff through a door in the back wall into an open area.

"You'll see our guest has a large ten-by-ten fenced-in area inside. There's a dog bed, sterilized after each guest leaves, along with the entire area. Scruff will also have a private door to the outside, which opens into a twenty-foot by twenty-foot run, all fenced in and separated from the other dogs."

He looked at Scruff, smiled, and said, "Do you think this will meet your needs, fella?"

Back in the reception area, he glanced at the book.

"Please remember to put down the time you'll be back for him," he said.

"The viewing won't be over until 9:00 this evening, so I guess I'll come for him at 10:00. Is that too late?"

"No, we offer 24-hour service here. We're one of the few that do," the attendant said.

Martha held Scruff tightly. Her heart sank as she heard him whine while she walked toward the door. This was good for him, and he needed to get used to it. He'd be here a lot in the next few days.

"It will only be for a few hours," she reassured him.

She returned to the motel and got ready.

She arrived at Green's Funeral Home at one o'clock. Harold Sr. had suggested the family come for a private viewing an hour before the public arrived. As she entered the viewing room, she felt like she was on display, like a portrait in a museum. Even though it was still early, many members of her father's family had already gathered.

On a small stand was the guest book, which already bore the names of many of her aunts and uncles.

She made her way to her mother's side and stood next to her and her sister, on the right side of the casket. Looking at her father lying in repose, she felt her face heat up. She buried her face in her hands.

"Are you okay, dear?" her mother whispered.

"I will be. Give me a minute."

After drying her tears, she turned toward the people. She knew her makeup was a mess, so she returned to the restroom to fix it.

The next hour passed painfully slow. One by one, the members of her dad's family filed by, many of whom she had only met once at a family reunion. But they all spoke of her father as if they had been his closest friends.

Before the family's hour was over, people started flooding into the room—church members, other pastors, and leaders from the community.

By the time she slipped away for dinner, she was exhausted. She returned an hour later, still drained. As she made her way through the crowd, she spotted Judy Phillips from the corner of her eye. She pivoted and looked toward her smiling face. Finally, someone she really knew.

"How are you holding up?" Judy asked.

"Okay, I guess," she answered. "But I can't wait for this to be over."

"I know you have a lot on your mind right now, but if you want, we could grab a late snack," Judy offered.

"It'll be really late," Martha said. "It'll be after ten o'clock before I can get away from here. Then I need to pick up Scruff."

"That's okay. You have my number. Call me," Judy replied.

"I've got to go," Judy added. "I'm supposed to work a couple of hours tonight for a friend so she can attend her son's ball game."

Martha worked through the throng until she returned to her sister and mother.

She continued to shake hands and smile until the muscles in her face ached. She caught herself glancing at her watch every few minutes.

So, this is what eternity feels like.

At the beginning of the evening, she tried to focus on each person as they came by, offering their words of sympathy. Many of the condolences were mixed with contempt for Jamal Richards. Many were hoping he would get the death penalty. It seemed strange to her to be discussing the death penalty at a funeral.

By the end of the evening, her response to each person had become a simple, "Thank you for your sympathy."

She called Judy, and they agreed to meet at McDonald's for a late snack. She picked up Scruff and took him to her room before meeting Judy.

Martha ordered a salad, and when the food arrived, she scarfed it down like she hadn't eaten in a week.

"You must really be hungry," Judy said, a mixture of amazement and amusement.

"I must have been hungrier than I thought," Martha replied.

After finishing her meal, they both ordered a cup of decaffeinated coffee.

"I can't know how you feel, losing your dad," Judy said. "And now you have to wait for the trial of that animal who murdered him. How do you do it?"

"How do I do what?" Martha questioned.

"How do you stay so calm? I'd be a basket case," Judy said.

"I never really thought about it," Martha replied. "It's just what happened, and I guess I have to live with it."

They moved to a lighter subject and talked about their friends from school. It shocked Martha to learn that the little girl with bright red curly hair and a face covered with freckles who sat behind her in science class was now a vice president at a large computer company.

The class geek was now the class hero. What a laugh. And Billy Davidson, the chubby short boy from English class, was now a world-renowned writer. In fact, she had read several of his books. She didn't know Billy had changed his name to William David. His last book had sold over a million copies.

It was midnight when she and Judy finally said goodnight and went home.

The evening had been extended, and Martha was happy to return to her motel room. With Scruff curled up at her feet, she fell asleep.

Chapter 4

Martha waited. She, her mother, and her sister sat in a room with several people she hadn't seen before. Among the familiar faces were Lt. Malroy and, of course, Ken Henderson.

A woman in a uniform escorted them from the room down a dark hall to a small space with just enough chairs for the group. The room had been painted entirely gray: the metal door, the cement floor, and the cinder block walls were all gray. Everywhere Martha looked, she encountered the bland, emotionless gray.

The only break in the monotony was the beige metal chairs and the black curtain behind the Plexiglas window in the center of the wall the chairs faced. Over the Plexiglas window was a large round clock with hands more extensive than usual. It was five minutes to twelve.

Martha watched, transfixed, as the black curtain parted in the middle and slowly opened, revealing another room. The white of the new space was brilliant in contrast to the dull gray. In the middle of the room was a medical table. To her right was an open door. Two guards walked in and began preparing the table.

They released a lever, tipping the table forward until it stood utterly vertical. Only then did she notice that the table also had arms extending.

After the table was ready, the door opened again. A guard entered, leading a priest, followed by a young African American man. The guards worked together, fastening the restraints and securing the young man to the table. A man in a black suit read the charges aloud:

"A jury of your peers found you guilty of murder in the first degree." He then asked the young man if he had anything to say.

Martha saw the terror in his eyes as fear of death overcame him. He cried uncontrollably.

"I did not do this!" he cried, tears streaming down his face. "I'm innocent. I don't want to die!"

Those words echoed in Martha's ears, *"I did not do this. I am innocent. I don't want to die."*

Her eyes snapped open. A cold sweat covered her body. It had been a nightmare. Martha turned on the light beside her bed, her body shaking, flushed, and nauseated. His look of terror was imprinted in her mind, and his voice continued to echo in the silence of her room.

It was 4:00 AM. She lay back down but couldn't sleep. The nightmare had been so vivid, so absolute. Around 5:30 that morning, she decided to find out what had happened to her father. She couldn't let her nightmare become a reality, no matter what Malroy wanted.

She took a notepad and pen from the motel's desk and began developing a plan. First, she would meet with the reporter who had written the article about Jamal Richards' arrest. Second, she would try to visit Richards herself. Finally, she would meet again with Ken Henderson for suggestions on how to proceed.

At 7:00 AM, she walked down to the Dinner Bell for breakfast. She was finishing her black coffee when Judy walked out.

"Are you okay?" Judy asked.

"I had a dream last night that Jamal might be innocent," Martha replied.

Judy frowned and crossed her arms. "Why do you think Jamal is innocent? Just because of a dream? Be careful. The police think Jamal is guilty, and I'm sure they know what's best."

Martha explained that she wanted to ensure an innocent man didn't suffer, but Judy had already decided about Jamal. She wasn't going to budge. Martha realized that no amount of argument would change

Judy's mind. Knowing it would be pointless, she excused herself, paid her bill, and returned to her room.

She didn't have time to worry about Judy. She had a funeral to prepare for.

"Back to the border with you, fellow," Martha said to Scruff.

He started whining as soon as Martha turned into the driveway of Canine Heaven.

"Don't start," she said. "You know you can't come to the funeral."

Chapter 5

"Where have you been?" Ruth asked as Martha walked through the door of the church.

"I had to take care of Scruff," Martha replied.

Ruth hurried Martha to the front of the church, where Rev. Joy, Pastor Rick, and her sister were waiting.

"As I was telling your sister and mother before you arrived, the funeral will take between fifty and sixty minutes," Rev. Joy said.

Martha sighed loudly.

"Too long?" he asked.

"No, I guess not," she answered.

Pastor Chris led the procession down the center aisle at precisely eleven o'clock. Behind him was Rev. Joy, the District

Superintendent, followed by Ruth, Mary, and Martha. Martha could feel the eyes of the people in the crowded church on her. She took a seat next to Mary. The silence was deafening as they waited.

Finally, Pastor Chris stepped up to the pulpit and began as Martha had heard her father begin funeral services many times.

"Dying Christ has destroyed our death, and rising Christ has restored our life..."

After a brief greeting, Pastor Chris read her father's eulogy. Martha remembered each of the parishes as Chris read them aloud. Each one had its own story. In Marystown, she and Mary were born. In Columbus, her mother and father had a rough time.

Father was often out late, smoothing ruffled feathers in the congregation. Then they moved to Brownsville. Things seemed to settle in Brownsville, and Dad was home most nights. The church there was more open to change.

Rev. Joy began the sermon, taking his text from Psalm 23. He had been a family friend for years, and they had attended seminary together. He shared some humorous stories about her father's dating life during seminary and how Dad always went for the "bad girl" types until Ruth made him settle down.

After the sermon, the choir sang two memorable songs, with Sister Lewis sobbing through both. In fifty-five minutes, the funeral was over, and Martha felt relief as Pastor Chris closed with prayer.

Ruth, Mary, and Martha left the funeral home and rode to the Brownsville Memorial Gardens in the black limousine. The graveside service was thankfully brief.

They all returned to the church for a meal provided by the congregation. It reminded Martha of what her father always said:

"After you die, they're going to put you in a box, put the box in the ground, and then everyone will go back to the church and eat potato salad." She scooped a heap of potato salad onto her plate and whispered, "Dad, you were right."

Senator Rick Phillips was one of the first people to approach her at the lunch. "Jamal Richards will get what he has coming," he said.

"Why do you think he did it?" Martha asked.

"Who else could have? His fingerprints were all over the house," Rick replied.

"Who told you that?" Martha asked.

"Well, Daniel— Daniel Malroy has been my friend for years. The case came up during our coffee meeting last week. Daniel assured me they had the right man. That's good enough for me."

"If they're sure," Martha said.

As a small group gathered around, Rick added, "As a leader in the community, I want to assure you I will not rest until they sentence Jamal Richards for this appalling act." Rick was a politician all the way.

"Martha, can you come over here? I have someone I want you to meet," Ruth called out.

Mercifully, Martha excused herself and retreated to her mother's side. It was late when she picked up Scruff.

"Believe me, you didn't miss a thing, Scruff," Martha said as he jumped into the front passenger seat.

She returned to the motel, slipped into her pajamas, fed Scruff, and turned on a movie. Before even the first commercial break, her eyes drifted shut.

Chapter 6

Martha couldn't shake the dream, even after the funeral. That morning, she returned to Mary's apartment. Mary was already up and dressed in bright pink—a radiant pink flowered blouse, light pink shorts, and a pink scarf holding her hair back. Yes, it was still December.

"Is the pink for cancer awareness?" Martha asked.

"Just felt like pink, no real reason," Mary replied. "Want a cup of coffee?"

"If there's any left," Martha said.

They entered the kitchen, and Martha poured herself a large mug of the dark brew.

"How do you feel about Dad's murder?" Martha began.

"Well, I hate it," Mary said. "Why do you ask?" "What if Jamal is innocent?" Martha asked.

"Innocent? Never!" Ruth said from the doorway.

"How do you know, Mom?" Martha replied.

"The police said so," Ruth answered. "And I just know."

"But what if the police are wrong?" Martha asked.

"I suppose it's possible," Mary said.

"Why did you bring this up?" Ruth asked.

Martha explained her dream and fears that an innocent man might be in prison.

"Because of a dream?" Ruth chided.

"Well, yes, and just a feeling, I guess," Martha confessed. "I just want to be sure."

"How can you be sure?" Mary asked.

"I guess I need to find out for myself," Martha said.

Mary smiled. "Playing detective? Count me in."

"Not a detective, just some conversations to see how we feel," Martha said.

Ruth sat down. "Waste of time."

"Well, it's our time to waste, right, Martie?" Mary said.

"Right, you are, sis. If we want to waste our time, it's our time," Martha agreed.

Ruth's face turned red, and she stomped out of the kitchen.

"So, where do we start?" Mary asked.

Martha, unsure where to begin, shrugged. She was no detective—she was a librarian.

"This calls for a trip to the library," Martha said.

As soon as they entered the library, the attendant turned toward them. "We're only open until three because of our Christmas Party."

Martha cringed. Mom would expect them to attend Christmas Eve services. Singing Christmas carols at a time like this felt immoral—celebrating so soon after her father's death.

She paused for a moment to take it all in. For some people, the sight of an ocean, a trip to the mountains, or a camping trip restores them. But for Martha, it was always an excellent book. To escape from her life for a few hours was rehabilitating.

"We could start with the newspaper reporter who wrote the story," Martha suggested.

She browsed through the newspapers until she found the one with the article about Jamal Richards from the Saturday paper. She looked at the byline and saw that the reporter's name was Sherry Porter. Martha continued to peruse past issues to see what other pieces Porter had written. She was a competent journalist, unlike some hacks.

A quick check of the phone book gave her the number for the *Brownsville Herald*. After a brief call, they had an appointment to meet Sherry Porter for a luncheon meeting the day after Christmas.

They agreed not to attend the Christmas Eve service. It was too soon.

Ruth opened her Bible and read, "In those days a decree went out from Caesar Augustus that all the world…" Her voice broke, and she burst into tears.

Martha took the Bible from her and closed it. "Maybe next year we'll be ready…"

No gathering around the tree. The tree was still at their house, and they didn't want to return there. It was just too painful for all of them. Christmas Eve and Christmas Day came and went. It didn't feel like Christmas this year.

Chapter 7

The coffee shop Sherry suggested was just a block from the *Herald's* office. Martha arrived twenty minutes before their scheduled meeting. There was no mistaking Sherry when she walked in. She was five foot ten, with shoulder-length brown hair, and dressed in a two-piece blue business suit that showed off her figure without being immodest. She entered the coffee shop like the owner, stopped inside the door, and surveyed the crowd. She marched purposefully over to Martha's booth in a few seconds and sat down.

In those few seconds, Martha had decided this was the woman she wanted to be. Sherry Porter exuded authority, magnetism, and charisma. Martha could easily picture Sherry barking orders at the other reporters, expecting them to follow without question. Sherry was no-nonsense— get in there and get the job done. Martha saw herself as anything but authoritative. She was a librarian, for God's sake—who would ever jump when she barked?

Martha began nervously, "Ms. Porter, thank you for agreeing to meet with me on such short notice." As she spoke, she felt knots forming in her stomach as she questioned why she was even there. She was a librarian, after all.

"Just call me Sherry," she said, pulling a thin file from her black leather briefcase and placing it on the table before them. "I brought copies of everything we have on file concerning your father's murder, along with the notes from my interview with Jamal. I think this is what you were looking for." She placed her hand authoritatively on the folder.

"You can have it if you agree to let me know what you find out," Sherry added.

"What makes you think we're going to find anything out?" Martha asked.

"Why else would you have asked to see me if you weren't looking into this matter?" Sherry asked. "Do we have an agreement?" Mary shook her head, and Martha shrugged.

Sherry slid the file across the table toward Martha. "Inside, you'll find copies of all the notes the other reporter took at the time of the murder and the stories we ran in the *Herald*."

Martha placed her hand on top of the file but hesitated before opening it. She flipped it open, and the first thing she saw was a photo. It was of her father, lying covered in his own blood on the floor of his study. A lump formed in her stomach and shot straight up to her throat. She had to swallow several times to keep from crying. She couldn't take her eyes off the picture. Her father, once so full of life, now sprawled on the floor, frozen in time, lifeless.

Files from his filing cabinet littered the floor, their contents flung haphazardly around his body. She wanted to look away. She desperately longed to divert her gaze, but the picture kept pulling her back.

Sherry sat silently, respectfully, almost reverently, waiting. Martha finally looked up from the photo into Sherry's eyes.

"You interviewed Jamal. What do you think about him?" Martha asked.

"What do I think?" Sherry replied.

"Do you think he did it?" Martha pressed.

"He claims he's innocent, but I don't know," Sherry said.

"If you were me, what would you do?" Martha asked, hoping for guidance.

"If I were you, I'd want to know for certain that he was guilty if it was my father. I'd talk to him myself. That's just what I would do," Sherry answered.

Sherry drained her glass of Diet Coke and then stood. "I hope what we've discussed helps you do the right thing. I just wish I knew what the right thing was. If you need my help, you know where to find me. Remember our deal."

As much as Martha dreaded the prospect, it was now clear she couldn't put her fears to rest until she met Jamal Richards face-to-face. Sherry had hit the nail on the head—it was the only right thing to do. But how could she get in to see him? She would need help— help that could only come from one place. He was the lead officer in this case.

Somehow, she had to convince Detective Malroy to arrange a visit for her. She did not look forward to meeting Malroy again, especially after the way their last meeting had ended.

Martha decided not to call Malroy but to visit his office in person.

She drove over to his office and waited.

"Mrs. Thomas, how may I help you?" he asked.

"I'd like to visit Jamal Richards," she replied.

His eyes grew cold and hard. "Why, may I ask?"

"I just want to talk to him. I need to ask him about my father's murder."

His nostrils flared. "What do you hope to learn?"

"I just need to make sure he's guilty."

"I don't think so," he said.

"Sherry Porter, the reporter for the *Herald*, might be interested in investigating a police force cover-up," Martha said. "You know, a frame job. I can see the headlines now."

She could see the tightening of his muscles, the glare in his eyes, and the crimson flush creeping up his neck. He was silent for a moment.

"I'll see what I can do," he said gravelly.

After a pause, he spoke through clenched teeth. "Okay, you can see him. I'll make the call today. Give me a number where I can reach you."

She jotted down her number and quickly left the room.

About an hour later, her phone rang. It was Malroy. He didn't wait for her to say hello. When she picked up the receiver, he said, "The prison expects you at ten tomorrow morning. Don't be late." He hung up.

Was that anger she heard in his voice? Or fear?

Chapter 8

Martha woke the following day to find snow falling all night, covering her Camaro with three inches of fresh, white powder. She searched her car in vain for an ice scraper, but there was no need for one back in San Antonio. She glanced at her watch—time was slipping away. She grabbed the CD jewel case of the one she had bought the night before, removed the CD, and placed it on the passenger seat. She scraped away the snow and ice from the windshield using the jewel case.

The makeshift tool worked well until she got to the back windows. As she forced the jewel case over the driver's side rear window, she felt the case give way, followed by the cracking of plastic. It shattered into pieces and fell into the snow at her feet.

She surveyed her work. She could see out the front and back, but her side vision was still limited. Climbing into the car, she started for the highway. The radio reported that the snow would keep coming, and the area was under a level-two snow emergency.

The announcer repeated, "If you do not have to be on the roads, this is a good day to stay home."

She spotted a convenience store and service station where she purchased a combination ice scraper and snow brush. After finishing cleaning off her car, she noticed the snowplows had cleared the highway, so she made good time. She drove fifty miles an hour until she reached the turnoff leading to the prison. The next ten miles were treacherous. The back road to the prison hadn't been plowed, so she drove slowly, trying to follow the path left by a four-wheel drive vehicle.

Martha pulled into the prison parking lot at ten. She had hoped to arrive earlier. She entered the main door, where a uniformed guard met her.

"Name and reason for your visit today?" he asked.

"Martha Thomas," she replied.

He flipped through the pages on his clipboard, then said, "Yes, Miss Thomas, we have you right here. Wait right there."

He disappeared through a gray metal door and returned with a husky female guard a few minutes later.

"Miss Thomas, please follow me," the female guard said curtly.

They went through another gray metal door, down a hall, into a room without windows and a small table in the center.

"According to our records," the female guard said, "Miss Thomas, you're here to see Jamal Richards. Inmate Richards is in Maximum

Security. Before you can see him, a complete search is required. Do you consent to this search?"

Martha hesitated. *What's a complete search?*

"I guess so," she replied.

The female guard handed her some forms and asked Martha to sign her full name in three places and initial them in two. She explained this was a consent form for the search.

After Martha signed, the guard walked to the door, glanced back, and said, "Part of the search requires you to remove all your clothing except your bra and panties. Just place your clothes on the table. I'll be back shortly with a witness for your protection. Please undress."

Martha complied, placing her clothes on the table and waiting. Forty-five minutes passed before the guard returned. Instead of a female guard, it was the male guard she had met earlier. Embarrassed, Martha tried to cover herself with her arms.

The female guard said, "I'm sorry, but all our female guards are unavailable. He's just here as a witness for your protection."

Without waiting for Martha to respond, she instructed, "If you will face the door and place your arms straight out from your sides, we can get this over."

Martha turned toward the male guard, her arms outstretched, and waited. The female guard roughly squeezed each of her breasts and continued for several seconds longer than Martha felt was necessary. Her fingers moved down Martha's body and rubbed her panties, both front and back. Martha's humiliation turned to anger. After a few more moments, the female guard said, "She's clean." The male guard left the room.

The female guard then slowly went through each article of clothing. Once finished, she said, "You may get dressed now," and watched as Martha redressed.

The guard led her down the hallway. As they walked, they passed a room with ten guards—half male and half female—drinking coffee and talking. The female guard glanced back at Martha and said, "They were unavailable; they're on break."

They approached an old wooden door with a large, frosted, beveled glass window at the top. In the center of the window, in gold lettering, was the word "Warden." The guard knocked and waited to be invited in. A voice from inside said, "You may enter."

The guard entered, appeared in front of a large oak desk, and said, "Sir, Ms. Thomas is here to see Inmate Richards." On the desk was a matching oak and brass nameplate: "Warden Gallinger."

Warden Gallinger was a balding man in his late fifties, wearing a brown three-piece suit, a white starched shirt, and a brown striped tie. "Miss Thomas, we've been expecting you. My good friend, Detective Malroy, called and said you'd be coming. He asked us to be of every courtesy to you. His exact words were, 'Make this a visit Miss Thomas will never forget.' I'm glad the snow didn't stop you this morning."

Now it all made sense—the strip search, the body probing, the male guard as a witness when there were female guards just around the corner. Malroy was behind it. He would do anything to stop her from seeing Richards.

"Officer Collier will be glad to take you to see Inmate Richards. You'll have fifteen minutes with him. Make the most of your time." Gallinger said.

"Officer Collier, will you escort Miss Thomas to visitor's room number ten?"

Collier led Martha deeper into the prison. They walked for what felt like miles until they reached another metal door. Collier opened the door and waited for Martha to enter. Nothing could have prepared her for what she saw. She had expected to meet the clean-cut, fresh-faced young African American man from the picture in the *Brownsville Herald*, a young man who looked around eighteen.

But the man sitting on the chair bolted to the floor was not what she had anticipated. In his early twenties, this man had shoulder-length dreadlocks peeking out under a bright red and white bandanna.

He wore an unbuttoned blue prison shirt, exposing a white V-neck T-shirt. He had rolled up the shirt's sleeves, and a pack of smokes was tucked into the left sleeve. Jamal looked more like a gang member than the person she had seen in the paper.

Martha entered the room, followed by Officer Collier.

"So, who are you, and why did you want to see me?" Jamal Richards asked.

Martha sat in the chair across from him and extended her hand to shake his. He just stared at her, his hand remaining flat on the table.

Officer Collier stepped forward and commanded, "No contact. Ms. Thomas, there will be no physical contact with the inmate." "Ms. Thomas," Jamal began, "You're related to—"

"I'm his daughter," Martha answered.

Jamal leaned forward, causing Collier to tense up.

"Look, lady," he said firmly, "I didn't kill your father. No one believes me, but I didn't do it."

She looked into his eyes, sensing something there that told her Jamal was telling the truth. She needed to gather as much information as possible in her fifteen minutes.

"If you didn't do it, how did your fingerprints end up in our house?" she asked.

Jamal paused before responding. "Why do you care? Everyone's already convinced I'm guilty. What difference does it make?"

She leaned in. "Honestly, I'm not sure. But what do you have to lose by telling me what happened that afternoon? Start at the beginning."

Jamal considered this and then began.

"I'd been looking for a chance to get away from here since I heard my mom was in the hospital. She lives in Columbus. That morning, I was working outside, clearing snow from the back parking lot, under the watch of Palmer, a guard here. He started feeling sick with the flu and said he was about to throw up, then ran to the restroom. That was my opportunity. I jumped the fence between the parking lot and the railroad tracks. I followed the tracks north. A couple of hours later, I came across your father's house. I came through the backyard. He let me in, gave me some clothes and money, and then I left."

Martha listened intently, observing every expression and mannerism as Jamal spoke, trying to decide whether he was lying or telling the truth.

She was also mentally building a timeline of events. When he finished, she said, "I'm not sure if I should believe you."

"Look, lady," Jamal insisted, "I didn't kill anyone. I'm telling the truth. I couldn't kill him. I wouldn't, any more than you could."

"What do you mean?" she asked.

"Never mind," Jamal muttered, looking away.

At that moment, Officer Collier stepped into the room and said,

"Ms. Thomas, your time is up." It hadn't been fifteen minutes yet, but Martha decided not to argue.

She might need to revisit Jamal, and she didn't want to burn any bridges. She stood, thanked Jamal for his time, and followed Collier through the maze of hallways until they reached the door leading her back into the world. She didn't breathe easily until she was safely in her car.

Martha began the treacherous ten-mile drive back to the highway. When she finally turned onto the main road, she sighed in relief. She believed Jamal, but she knew the only way to convince Detective Malroy of his innocence was to find the real killer. The thought of facing a murderer sent a chill down her spine. This wasn't *Matlock* or *CSI*. There was no safety of a television screen separating her from the danger. But she couldn't let an innocent man suffer, even if he looked like a member of a gang.

Her training had been as a librarian, not as a crime specialist. What could she do? The library. She drove straight to the Brownsville

Library, walked to the first open computer terminal, and began her search. In the dialog box, she typed "CRIMINAL INVESTIGATION." She watched as a row of small squares ran across the bottom of the screen, processing thousands of resources to find relevant information. In seconds, it displayed ten possible texts.

She jotted down the titles of two books and quickly determined they were on the second floor. She climbed the stairs and grabbed the first book listed: *Follow the Clues: Go Along with the Police from Investigation to Court.* This one seemed promising.

She then picked up the second book, *Inside the Criminal Mind.* As she turned the book over, she froze. There, staring back at her from the dust cover, was the face of Detective Malroy. A younger Malroy, with a fuller head of hair, but it was unmistakably him. She had never imagined she would be confronted by his image in a book about criminal investigation. When Ken had said Malroy could write a book on the subject, he hadn't been joking.

Here it was—over three hundred pages of proof. Malroy was a crime scene expert, which raised the question: why was a crime scene expert working in a small town like Brownsville? The back cover revealed that he had been a professor of Criminal Justice at the University of Cincinnati.

She checked out both books and returned to her motel room, where she spent the rest of the evening poring over them and taking notes.

"Scruff, I hate to say this, but Malroy knows his stuff. His step-by-step field guide is outstanding. He's also a talented author and a great communicator. So why is he here in Brownsville and not teaching at UC? We have to find out, Scruff."

The following day, she dressed and started for Mary's apartment. *Freezing rain. Just what she needed this morning.*

The Camaro slid as she pushed down on the gas pedal, carefully pulling out onto the highway.

"Better take it easy, Scruff," she said as she accelerated slowly.

A black SUV came up behind her and passed. She slowed even more to let it get around. As the SUV came up beside her, it swerved and slammed into her front bumper.

She heard the sickening sound of metal against metal, followed by the crunch of gravel as the tires bit into the side of the road. She fought the steering wheel hard to keep the car on course. The SUV pulled back into its lane. It must have hit black ice and lost control.

But then it came over on her again—this time, harder. She tried to steady the car, but the SUV was too big and powerful. She felt the car lose control and veer off the road.

She was propelled downward, bouncing around and slamming her head. The car finally came to a stop when it hit a giant oak tree. A branch broke through the windshield, pulverizing the passenger seat.

"Scruff!"

She tried to wipe the sweat from her face, only to pull back her hand, covered in blood. She felt everything closing in on her as dizziness overwhelmed her.

"Scruff!"

***

"Are you alright, my dear?" Ruth's trembling voice cut through the fog. "Wake up, dear. I can't lose you too."

Martha slowly slid her eyes open, hearing her mother's voice.

She saw blue walls and a television set centered on the wall. She turned slightly and saw windows looking out onto a parking lot.

"Where am I?" Martha asked weakly.

"Oh, you're alright. You're in the hospital," Ruth said, relieved.

"Hospital? But why?" Martha aske, confused.

"Martie, are you alright?" Mary asked, her voice full of concern.

Her mind cleared, and she looked up to see Officer Ken Henderson, in full uniform, standing at the foot of her bed.

Mary took her hand. "Hey, Martie, I asked if you were okay." "I… I think so," Martha replied.

"Our investigation has concluded that you were in an accident with a hit-and-run driver, Ms. Thomas," Ken said, glancing at an aluminum clipboard. "Someone slid on the ice and side-swiped you, then you lost control and went off an embankment."

"Oh, Scruff, what happened to Scruff?" Martha hated how attached she'd become to the mutt.

"He's fine," Ruth said, reassuringly touching Martha's shoulder.

"We have him at the apartment."

"He hid in the car's floorboard when we removed the branch. He was curled up, whimpering, and has a few minor scratches, but he's in good health," Ken added.

"Martie, Martie, what happened, Martie?" Mary repeated, her voice frantic.

Martha glanced up at her sister, then at Ken. "I remember driving toward your apartment when a big black truck, like a Tahoe, tried to pass me. Then, out of nowhere, it came over on me…"

"That's when we think he lost control for the first time," Ken said.

"Then he seemed to correct, but he came back over on me." "That's when he lost control the second time," Ken said.

"Mom, would you go find a nurse and see if I can have something to eat?" Martha asked, changing the subject.

"Sure, dear," Ruth said, leaving the room.

Once Martha was sure her mother was out of earshot, she said, "This didn't feel like an accident."

"What do you mean?" Ken asked.

"He hit me on purpose," Martha said, her tone serious.

"What makes you say that?"

"He was waiting for me. I saw him in the motel parking lot but thought little of it. Then, when he came up beside me, he looked right at me and smiled."

"He smiled?" Ken asked, surprised.

"I thought he was flirting, but then he turned the wheel and approached my car. At first, I thought he lost control like you said, but there was no ice when he came over the second time. It was deliberate."

"Well," Ken said, "that changes everything. Can you think of any reason someone would do this to you?"

Mary stood there, her mouth hanging open, saying nothing. Ruth returned with a nurse.

"Can we talk later?" Martha said to Ken. "I'm feeling exhausted now."

"Sure," he said. "I'll check in with you tomorrow morning."

"Great," Martha said, turning toward the nurse. "Could I have a little snack before my nap?"

"Well, it's just past lunchtime. How about I make sure you get one of our lunches?" the nurse said, and before Martha could answer, she left the room.

Martha convinced Ruth and Mary to go home and rest, as they both looked frazzled.

"Here you go, dar-lynn," the nurse said, setting the brown hospital tray on Martha's table.

She thought hospitals must get a discount on these trays since they seemed to use them everywhere—from Columbus to Texas.

Different hospitals, same trays. Hopefully, it won't be the same food.

The bland fare, no salt, no sugar, no taste.

After lunch, she lay there, questioning again why she was so determined to find the truth. No one else seemed to care. Malroy and Henderson were happy that Jamal was guilty. Ruth certainly didn't want her following up on Jamal. Ruth became angry every time Martha mentioned his name. Sweet and innocent, Mary didn't care one way or the other; she was just along for the ride.

About an hour later, the nurse returned for the tray.

"Are we all finished, dar-lynn?" she asked, picking it up and leaving the room.

At about 6:00, the door opened, and a short Arabian man walked in.

"Hi, my name is Husam Abdil. I'm your doctor. You had a nasty accident. We had to fix your head and stop the bleeding."

"Can I go home now?" Martha asked.

"No, we want you to stay overnight for observation. If all goes well, you'll go home tomorrow," he replied.

With that, he left the room.

Martha closed her eyes. It had been a long day, and she was ready for sleep.

Chapter 9

"Wake up," said a male voice.

She opened her eyes, expecting to see Ken, but it was a male nurse wearing a surgical mask.

"I came to give you something to help you sleep."

"But I was asleep," Martha protested.

The nurse injected a syringe of clear liquid into her I.V.

"Smart girls stay home and keep their noses out of things that don't concern them," the nurse said, pulling down the mask. Martha saw it was the same man who had run her off the road.

"Now, you sleep because you will wake up... this time." Martha felt the effects of the sedative take over.

"You don't want us to come back. If we can get to you here, we can get to you anywhere."

He stood there, petting her head like a small, helpless animal, as she drifted to sleep. She could not stay awake.

"Good girl, now stay that way."

Martha called Ken as soon as she woke from her deep sleep. When he arrived, she told him about her nocturnal visitor.

"Are you sure that's what he said?" Ken asked.

"Those are the words I remember, yes."

"Let me talk to the head nurse. We need to find this man."

Ken left the room and returned a few moments later, the nurse trailing behind him. Ken looked at the head nurse and said, "Repeat what you told me."

"I'm sorry, Miss, but we don't have any male nurses here."

"On this floor?" Martha asked.

"No, in this hospital, no male nurses are employed." "Thank you. You can go now," Ken said.

"Sorry, dear," the head nurse said, turning for the door.

"Wait a second. Do you have video cameras in the hallways?" Martha asked.

"Yes, we record them in our security department," the nurse answered.

"Great. We need to see that video," Martha said, sitting up in the bed.

"Just a minute, young lady. You're a patient, so you'll stay right there until Doctor Abdil releases you," the nurse said.

"I'll check it out. You stay right here in bed. If I find anything, I'll come tell you," Ken said.

As he opened the door, he glanced back at her and winked. "Here's looking at you, kid."

Who was this man? What did he want? Why did he say "we"? "If we can get to you here... Who was the *we?*"

Ken was gone for about half an hour. "They have him on video. For what good it will do us, he must have known the placement of the cameras. He avoided all but one; then he put his head down. We never saw his face," Ken said.

"So, we have nothing," Martha said.

"Maybe not. I'm having a copy of the video sent to the station. We'll send it to the State Police to see if they can get something from it."

"I want out of here. I don't feel safe," Martha said.

"Is that the same I.V. you had last night?" Ken asked.

"Yes, they haven't changed it. Why?"

"I want to send it to the lab to find out what he injected into you."

"I'm sure the nurse can help with that," Martha said.

She felt safe with Ken around. She was sure it was because he was a police officer... well, almost sure that was why.

The head nurse returned with Ken. "The doctor said you won't need this anymore," she said as she pulled the needle from Martha's arm.

Ken placed the I.V. needle and hose in a brown paper bag and folded the top down.

"This is going to the lab later today."

"I hope to get out of here this morning," Martha said.

Around noon, Doctor Abdil entered her room. "You can go home now. You don't need to stay in the hospital any longer. I'll sign you out now."

"Thank you. I'll call for a ride," Martha said.

Ruth and Mary arrived about thirty minutes later.

"Here's your wheelchair, Ms. Thomas," the head nurse said, wheeling it into the room.

"I don't need a wheelchair. I can walk out on my own." "I'm sorry, it's hospital policy," the nurse said.

"Where do I need to go to pick her up?" Mary asked.

"Please, just pull up under the overhang in front. We'll be there in just a few minutes."

Mary left to get the car.

Ruth and the head nurse escorted Martha to the door.

"Now, you be careful. We don't want you back with us," the nurse said.

Martha sat down in the passenger seat of Mary's car and pivoted into the seat.

"Please take me home," Martha said.

"How about going to my apartment instead?" Mary said, laughing.

"Texas is too far away."

It was an uneventful drive to the apartment, even though Martha kept looking for a black Tahoe on every corner. After arriving home, Ruth changed into her housecoat and lay on the sofa for a nap. Mary and Martha retreated to the kitchen.

"I'll make a pot of coffee, then we need to talk," Mary said.

"Okay."

"Now," Mary said, glancing into the living room to see their mother sleeping soundly, "tell me what happened last night."

Martha recounted the events of her nighttime visit again.

"What are you going to do, Martie?"

"I don't know, but it appears we've ruffled some feathers," Martha said.

"This could be really dangerous," Mary said. "Are you sure it's worth it?"

"If there wasn't something wrong, I don't think they'd come after me, whoever 'they' are," Martha said.

"But, sis, you could end up dead," Mary said. "Both of us could end up dead."

"I know, but what choice do we have?" Martha said.

"We could just forget it," Mary said.

"I couldn't live with myself if an innocent man went to prison because I did nothing."

"I guess you're right," Mary agreed. "But Mom won't like this." "I know, but then again, what else can I do?" Martha said.

"Are you going to keep going?" Ruth said from the other room.

"We thought you were asleep," Mary said.

"I beg you, don't continue. This won't end well," Ruth said.

"But, Mom, we have to," Martha said.

"You're going to regret it, I promise. Just let it go," Ruth said.

"I can't," Martha said.

"Remember, I warned you that you could find something that will break your heart," Ruth said.

"Wherever it leads, I have to know the truth," Martha said.

Ruth rolled back over.

Chapter 10

Martha and Mary developed their approach over several cups of coffee.

"First, we need to go through Dad's stuff—look at his calendar and see if we can get into his computer," Martha said.

"I don't know, sis. That seems wrong as if we're invading his space."

"How else can we find out what this is all about? We have to do something."

"I know, but looking at his calendar, computer, and life, it feels... wrong. Like we're being bad," Mary said.

Martha smiled and said, "But I thought you liked being bad."

"I do, most of the time."

"That settles it. Let's see what we can find out in Dad's study," Martha said.

Their father's study was across town, in the home they had shared for years. A dried bloodstain in the center of the room greeted them as they opened the old oak door to his office. They stood and stared for a moment before entering. This had been their father's sanctuary. On the back wall were three black metal filing cabinets. In front of them was an old, well-worn, second-hand desk their dad had picked up at an auction years ago.

He'd been so proud of that desk. "Got it for a steal," he would tell everyone. "That desk holds all my secrets," he would say with a sly smile to visitors.

Framed jerseys from Johnny Bench and Pete Rose adorned the back wall, along with a baseball signed by the Big Red Machine— their father's pride and joy. In the center of the desk sat a new HP computer.

"This is as good a place to start as any," Martha said, pushing the button to turn it on. The computer hummed, and a screen popped up, asking for a password.

"What do you think it might be?" Martha asked Mary.

"Try his birth date. It's just four numbers, so just the month and day," Mary suggested.

Martha typed in 0205 and pressed enter.

The computer hummed and opened to the desktop.

"Where do we go now?" Mary asked, peering over Martha's shoulder and leaning forward to focus on the screen.

"I guess we need to find his calendar."

After a few more keystrokes, a calendar appeared.

"It looks like Dad had only a few appointments in the weeks before his death," Martha said. "Here, look—he had a meeting every Thursday evening with someone, but there's no name or any details." She paused. "And he had an appointment with R. Phillip, with 'one week' written after it."

"And who or what is Bubbles?" Mary asked. "He's been meeting with Bubbles every Saturday at 2:00 for six weeks."

"This isn't much help, but I want to make some notes anyway," Martha said, pulling a stack of Post-it notes from the desk's top drawer. She wrote "Thursday evening" and then the word "Bubbles." She circled it. "I think this might be important."

As she opened the drawer to put the pad of Post-its back, she saw her father's checkbook.

"It's worth a look," Martha said.

"Should we? That's private," Mary said.

Martha opened the checkbook and flipped to the register. She read the names of the recipients: electric, cable, and gas companies, the local grocery store, and, of course, the church—nothing unusual. But then, there was a name they didn't expect: Sarah Richards. Her name came up every two weeks. Twice a month, Sarah Richards received a check for three hundred dollars.

"Do you see this?" Martha asked.

"Yeah, but who is Sarah Richards?" Mary said.

"Is she related to Jamal? If so, how?" Martha said, raising her eyebrows.

"The better question is why Dad was sending her money?" Mary said, slamming her fist into the desk. "And how long has this been going on?"

Martha pulled the Post-it note from her pocket and wrote in large capital letters: "SARAH RICHARDS."

"Should we ask Mom about her?" Martha asked.

"I'm not sticking my hand into that hornet's nest. You can," Mary said.

"If we don't ask Mom, we need to ask Sarah herself," Martha said.

"But first, I want to make a call."

Martha dug around in her purse and pulled out Malroy's card.

"You're not calling him, are you?" Mary said.

Martha silently dialed her iPhone.

"How can I help you?" came the cheerful, southern voice on the other end.

"May I speak to Officer Ken Henderson?" she asked.

Mary smiled and nodded. "Good call," she whispered in her sister's ear.

"Officer Ken Henderson, who am I speaking with?" came the voice on the other end.

"This is Martha Thomas. I was wondering if you could check something for me."

"I'll help you if I can."

"Can you check Jamal's record and see if there's any mention of

Sarah Richards?"

"I don't have to check. Sarah is Jamal's mother."

There was silence on the line.

"Are you there?" Ken asked.

"Yes, I'm just processing what you just said," Martha replied. "While I have you on the phone, the lab results are back, and they found that he injected you with morphine."

"Morphine?"

"That's what the lab said," Ken confirmed. "So, be careful from now on. This is serious."

"Can you get me a number for Sarah?" Martha asked.

"Why?"

"I'll let you know if I find anything out, I promise," Martha said.

"Hold on a moment," Ken said.

He returned a few minutes later with the number. Martha dialed the number and put her phone on speaker mode.

"Sarah Richards," came the voice on the other end.

"Hi, my name is Martha Thomas. I was hoping we could meet soon."

"Ask her about the money," Mary whispered in her ear.

"My sister and I have some questions for you."

There was a long sigh on the other end. "I've been expecting your call. Would you like to come here, or would you prefer I come to you?"

They agreed to meet at Sarah's home. Sarah gave them her address on the northeast side of Columbus.

Martha and Mary piled into the rental car and drove.

"What do you think she's like?" Mary asked.

"I don't know."

"Well, do you think she's beautiful or an old hag?"

"I don't know."

"I hope she's ugly, like the Wicked Witch."

"Or maybe like Broom-Hilda," Martha said. "You know, the green witch with the wart on her nose." They both laughed.

"She might greet us with, 'I'll get you and your little dog too,'" Mary said.

Scruff, who had been sleeping in the backseat, whined.

"Don't worry, fella, I won't let the mean, old, green witch get you," Martha said.

They continued on to Columbus, talking and laughing along the way.

They were creeping down the road, staring at mailboxes and scanning for the number.

"There it is: 2801 Overcourt Drive," Mary said.

It was a nice, one-story home in the center of a middle-class neighborhood, though unkempt. The grass needed mowing, and the hedges needed trimming, but it looked like a nice place to live.

"What are you going to say?" Mary asked.

"I think I'll start with, 'Hello,'" Martha answered.

They rang the doorbell, and Sarah answered.

She was no Broom-Hilda. Her caramel-colored skin shone with health, and her facial features were almost perfect. She had beautiful, curly brunette hair flowing over her shoulders. There was no other way to put it: Sarah was stunning.

"Would you like to come in?" Sarah asked politely.

She invited them into a large, mint-colored room with hardwood floors. The furnishings were elegant but simple and lived-in.

"I'm sure you have many questions for me," Sarah began. "But first, how about some tea or coffee?"

She was friendly, Martha thought. Too nice.

Sarah returned moments later with coffee for everyone.

"So, what would you like to know?" she said, setting the serving tray on the glass-topped coffee table and handing each of them a cup.

"Oh, do either of you need cream or sugar?"

"I could use a little of both," Mary said.

Sarah returned from the kitchen with a creamer and sugar set that matched the cups.

"Well, how can I help you?" Sarah asked sweetly.

Martha wanted to hate this woman, but she was making it impossible.

"Tell us about your relationship with our father," Martha said.

Sarah sat down and sighed.

"Yeah, and why did he send you money?" Mary added.

"It all started over 20 years ago. Your father was the pastor of a church here in Columbus. My husband, Marvin, died in a motorcycle accident. Your father agreed to do the funeral for me because I had no money. He was so kind and caring."

"We know he was kind and caring. What about the money?" Mary pressed.

"I'm getting there. We were in his study at the church when I broke down weeping. He sat down beside me to comfort me. I fell onto his shoulder. He put his arm around me... then."

"Then what?" Mary asked.

Martha had already figured it out.

"I knew it was wrong, and so did he, but we just couldn't stop. Holding moved to kissing, petting, to... well, you know."

"No, we don't know," Mary said.

"They had sex," Martha said.

Sarah's face flushed, and she smiled. "No, dear, we didn't just have sex. We made love."

Mary gagged and ran out the front door. "I think I'm going to be sick."

"I need to be with my sister," Martha said, following her.

Martha held Mary on the front porch as they both cried. Martha saw her father was not perfect for the first time. He made mistakes—big, mega mistakes. After they composed themselves, they returned to Sarah.

"So, how long did this affair go on?" Martha asked.

"Until you moved to Brownsville. He told me he couldn't do it anymore. He wanted to repair his marriage."

"So, why did Dad continue to send you money?" Mary asked.

"I told your father he didn't have to do it. I'm a vice president in a law firm, making good money, but he insisted. He said it was for Jamal."

"Why did he send money to Jamal?" Mary asked.

"Because Jamal is his son, right?" Martha said.

"Right, Jamal was our child. Your father visited every Thursday to be with Jamal."

"And you?"

"To visit, yes, nothing more. After he moved to Brownsville, we have never been... intimate."

"So, wait a minute. Jamal is our dad's son? That means he's..."

"Yes, Jamal is your half-brother," Sarah affirmed.

Mary looked at Martha. Mary's mouth dropped open, her eyes enlarged, her eyebrows arched.

"We have a brother?" Mary asked.

"A half-brother," Sarah answered.

"So, Jamal was at your father's house because he was also his father. He didn't go there to kill him. He was in trouble and just went to his father for help," Sarah said.

"Why didn't he tell the police about it?" Martha asked.

"Because no one knew Jerry was Jamal's father. He didn't want to hurt you or your mother."

"But he could end up in prison for life," Martha said.

"He'll do it if it keeps you and your family from being embarrassed in the community you had grown up in," Sarah said.

"But now, it has to come out. He can't go to prison for something he didn't do," Martha said.

Sarah's face, which had shone earlier, now became gloomy.

"Will you please talk to him? Talk some sense into him. That place is not good for him. He just told me on the phone that three guys jumped him, and he's in the hospital."

"Sure," said Martha and prepared to leave, her mind still racing with a thousand questions. The drive home was silent for the first thirty minutes.

Mary said, "Wow, I never expected that."

"I always felt Dad was hiding something, but this," Martha said.

"He was a cad, but he had good taste," Mary said. "Sarah is a looker."

Martha knew she would have to see Malroy and to arrange another visit with Jamal.

The words Jamal had said now made sense. "I could no more kill him than you could."

He was their father. She was certain now that Jamal had not killed their father, but how to prove it.

She did not want to, but she called Malroy as soon as they were home.

"Detective Malroy here. Who am I talking to?"

"This is Martha Thomas-"

"Well, little lady, what can I do to help you?"

"I would like to go visit Jamal again. I know you said-"

"No problem. Would you like to go tomorrow? What time would be good for you?"

"What did you say?"

"No problem. What time is good for you?"

"Ten?" Martha said.

"Great, I will call and set it up. Anything else I can do for you?"

"No, not that I can think of."

"Well, sweetie, never hesitate to call," Malroy said.

"Did you call?" Mary asked.

"Yes, and Malroy was, well, nice."

"Nice, Malroy? I did not think he knew the meaning of the word." Mary said.

"He called me, 'Little lady, and sweetie,'"

"Malroy?" Mary said.

Martha and Mary drove through an early morning snow fall, less than an inch, but deep enough to leave tire tracks. They drove to CCI, Cedartown Correctional Institute.

"I am not going into that place," Mary said.

"Why?" Martha said.

"Prisons are scary places. I watched prison movies. I will never go into a place like that."

"We are just visiting."

"YOU are just visiting. I'm staying here in the car."

***

"May I help you?" the guard at the desk asked.

"I am Martha Thomas-"

"Ms. Thomas, we have been waiting for you." Great, here comes the crucible.

"This way Ms. Thomas, the Warden Gallinger would like to talk to you."

Instead of the maze, this time they only made one turn, and they were in front of the Warden's office.

"Good morning, Ms. Thomas," Gallinger opened a file in front of him, "You are here to see inmate Richards again."

"I was told that inmate Richards had an accident following your last visit, and he is now in the infirmary. What happened?" Martha asked.

"He must have tripped and fallen down some stairs. Prison can be a dangerous place, Ms. Thomas."

"Is he okay?"

He stared at the file. "Yes, it appears he is doing fine, for now."

"Officer Collier, will you escort our guest to the infirmary?"

They left the office, and Collier led Martha through the massive complex of buildings until they came to a building marked "INFIRMARY."

Collier opened the door and led the way down a spotlessly clean, narrow hallway to a large, white door with a stenciled sign, "Ward 3." Inside were six beds, three on one wall, and three opposite them.

In the middle bed on the right-hand side was Jamal. They had bandaged his head, his left arm was in a cast, and his right leg elevated.

Her eyes widened, and her jaw dropped. "What happened to you?"

Jamal smiled at the guard, "I fell down the stairs... the same day you visited me."

I caused this.

"What do you want?"

"I spoke to your mother."

"I know, she told me."

"So?" she asked.

"So what? Now you know your father was my father. What difference does that make?"

"Did you do it?"

"My answer is still no!"

"So why will you not talk to me?"

Pointing to his cast and leg, "Duh."

"Someone did this because you talked to me," Martha said.

"No, I fell down some stairs, like I said. Just leave. It would be better for me if you did not come back."

"I think this visit is over," Jamal said to the guard.

Martha walked, and worried, as she returned to the car.

"Mary, what are you doing?"

Mary had kicked off her shoes on the passenger side of the car, propped her foot up on the dash, and painted her nails a bright purple.

"Just painting my toenails to match the streaks in my hair.'

"You don't have purple streaks,"

"Not yet," Mary said, laughing.

"Well," Mary said.

"Well, what?"

"What did he say about being our brother? It still makes my skin crawl."

"He admitted he was dad's son,"

"Duh, what else did he say?" Mary asked.

"Nothing. The guard was listening. Someone beat him up the last time I was here."

"Maybe we should forget this. Maybe it is for the best. If he is not-guilty, the courts will find it out," Mary said.

"I read an article that said a man spent twenty years behind bars for a crime he did not commit."

"Twenty years? That is a long time, but what can you do? What can we do?"

"I don't know, but I am going to find out," Martha said. "I do not want Jamal to spend twenty years in prison if he is innocent."

"Can we stop by the drugstore? I need to pick something up," Mary said.

Mary came out with three candy bars and a box of purple hair color.

***

Martha knew she had to do something, but what? I do not solve crimes, I read about them. But what had she read? The best approach was to go back to the beginning.

She dug around in her purse until she found the post-it-note she had created in her father's study.

As she read over it a second time, she tried to remember when she had heard her father used the name Bubbles. Was it the name of a person, a place, a thing? Bubbles, it had to have some meaning.

R. Phillips was the second note that she turned her attention to.

She pulled her phone from her handbag and typed his name into a web search.

She dialed the number.

"Senator Rick Phillips' office, how may I direct your call?" said a highly professional voice.

"My name is Martha Thomas, and I would like to speak with Senator Phillips."

"Ms. Thomas, let me check and see if Senator Phillips is available."

"Senator Phillips here, how can I help you?"

"Senator Phillips, this is Martha Thomas. I was wondering if I could get an appointment to see you. I have something I would like to discuss with you."

"Sure Martha, we've known each other for years. You don't need to call me Senator. I will always be Rick to you. Would today at 4 o'clock work for you?"

"Yes, 4 o'clock would be great."

She drove over to her sister's apartment where she found Mary, wearing a neon purple blouse, purple shorts, and now purple streaks in her strawberry- blond hair.

"Well, what do you think?"

"Mary, it looks different."

"I told you I was going to do it."

"I know. I guess I did not expect it to be so drastic. Bright purple?"

"I know. Don't you just love it?"

Martha wrinkled her brow, and screwed her lips together, "Like I said, it is different."

Martha and Mary drove toward Columbus.

"Do you remember Dad ever using the word, Bubbles?" Martha said.

"I have been thinking about it, and it seems he called someone that as a nickname, but I cannot remember who," Mary said.

"I remember. He had nicknames for all of us," Martha said.

Martha searched her memory. She also remembered him using the nickname, but could not recall for whom.

They arrived at Rick Phillips' office building, a massive skyscraper on High Street in downtown Columbus, the heart of the business section.

They rode the elevator to the penthouse suite.

The receptionist ushered them into his lavish office, lined with cherry bookcases, a huge, over-stuffed sofa, and chairs on one side, and a massive cherry desk dominating the center of the room.

This was impressive, not bad for a former mayor of Brownsville. Rick sat behind the desk, smiling that fake politician's smile.

"How can I help you, ladies?" he asked.

"We don't want to take a lot of your time. We know you are a remarkably busy man, but we had a question about an appointment you had with dad. Dad had an appointment with you two weeks ago.

Can you tell us what it was about?" Martha said.

"Let me see," he said, turning to his computer, typing a few seconds, "Yes, your father, and I were talking about the reception for Judy's wedding. He wanted to make sure we had the caterer lined up."

"Why did he write 'one week' beside your name?" Martha asked.

"He said he would like me to call him in one week to give him the name of the caterer for his files. Which I did."

"Well, I think that will do it," Mary said.

Martha was reluctant to leave, but Mary insisted.

After they were back in the car, Martha said, "He was lying." "Why do you say that?" Mary asked.

"Dad never cared about caterers or the receptions. He always said, 'the church is my concern, after you leave is your concern,' remember?"

"Now that you mention it, but why would he lie?"

"Why indeed?"

While driving home, Martha's phone rang.

"Hello."

"Martha, this is Judy Phillips. Are you busy?"

"I am driving. What can I do for you?"

"Remember me telling you about Billy Davidson, the writer? We are getting together at his place. The old gang from high school will be there. I wondered if you and your sister might like to join us?"

"When and where?"

"I will call you with all the info later tonight, toodles."

"I will wait for your call."

Martha hung up and said, "Mary, that was Judy, Judy Phillips."

"You mean the Senator's daughter."

"Yes, it just seems strange she would call now."

"What did she want?" Mary asked.

"She wanted to invite us to a get together with our old high school gang."

"Wow, when?"

"She is to call me," Martha said.

"I cannot wait. It has been years since I have seen them," Mary said.

"Were you ever invited to anything like this before?" Martha asked.

"Never, this is so cool,"

"Never, but minutes after our visit to the Senator, we get the call?" Martha said.

"Yes, I guess, but I will be outstanding. What should I wear? Look, me asking you. You never make a bold statement, and this calls for bold, the bolder, the better."

The bolder the better. What could that mean? She was afraid of Mary going bold. She had no restraint button.

That evening, Judy called back. She invited Mary and her to

Billy's home that Saturday for a party with the old gang. She gave Martha the time and the address.

There would be lots of food, and all the beer you can drink, she promised. Martha agreed to attend, even though she was a one beer gal.

Why a party? Why now? Did it have anything to do with her recent visit to her father's office? What was this all about? Could she trust Judy?

Chapter 11

Martha and Mary arrived at Billy's house—if you could even call it a house. From the road, it looked more like a mansion, something out of Hollywood rather than Brownsville.

As they pulled in, a valet stood waiting to take their keys. Martha hesitated, feeling embarrassed as she handed over the keys to her new rental.

"Oh, cool, a parker guy," Mary said, clearly impressed.

"A valet," Martha whispered, correcting her sister.

A man in starched jeans with a muscular build approached them. "Ladies, if you'll follow me," he said.

He led them up a well-maintained walkway to a large oak door, which a young woman in a maid's uniform opened.

The inside was as grand as the outside.

A young, fit man broke away from a group gathered in the dining area and headed straight toward them.

"Do you remember me?" he asked.

"I don't think so," Martha replied.

"I'm Billy Davidson."

"Billy? The last time I saw you, you were…"

"I know," he interrupted. "I wore glasses, was short, and chubby…"

"I wouldn't say chubby," Martha said, recalling the boy who was always in the library, reading.

"It's okay," Billy said with a grin. "After college, I lost weight, and I had Lasik."

"I did too—or at least the Lasik," Martha said with a smile.

Billy and Martha began walking together, leaving Mary to find her way.

"So, you're the famous William David. I think I've read all your books," Martha said.

"Oh, I hope not," Billy replied with a chuckle. "My first few books were disasters. While learning the craft, I had to give them away just to build a readership. But enough about me—what about you?"

"I became a librarian."

"You always loved books. You were always reading," Billy said.

"Maybe I read too much," Martha admitted.

"Never say that to a writer," Billy teased. "We make our living off people who read too much." They both laughed.

"Where are you living now?" Billy asked.

"I have a one-bedroom apartment in San Antonio."

"Do you like it there?"

"It's okay—no winters like you have around here," Martha replied.

Just then, a few other guests came around the corner.

Billy stood up. "I need to play host, but let's catch up before you leave."

Judy came over and sat beside Martha.

"Isn't he dreamy?" Judy asked.

"Who?" Martha replied.

"Billy, of course."

"I guess so," Martha said, glancing at him—and noticing that he was glancing back at her.

"I've never seen him do that before," Judy said.

"Do what?"

"Leave everyone else and talk to just one person, like he did with you," Judy said, smiling knowingly.

"Oh, Judy, really?" Martha said, shaking her head.

"No, seriously. He doesn't do that with anyone," Judy insisted.

During the meal, Billy made sure Martha sat beside him.

Between bites of hamburgers, Martha asked, "How did you start writing?"

"Your father had much to do with it," Billy replied.

"My dad? Really?"

"I asked him to read my first story, and he said he liked it. Then he started calling me 'Graphy.'"

"I remember that! But why 'Graphy?'"

"He said it was from the Greek word for 'writer.' Every time he called me that, it encouraged me to keep going," Billy explained.

"That's really cool," Martha said. "So, did you send him any royalties?" she joked.

"He encouraged me, but I had to do all the writing," Billy said with a laugh.

"Can I ask you something?" Billy said.

"Sure."

"Why did your dad call you 'Red?' You don't have red hair or wear red clothes. I never understood it."

"Oh, he wasn't calling me 'Red.' He was calling me 'Read'—R-EA-D. Whenever someone mentioned a book, I'd always say, 'Oh, yes, I've read that.'"

"So, it was 'Read,' not 'the color red,'" Billy said, laughing.

"Exactly."

"He had nicknames for all of us," Billy said. "I remember hanging out at your house every weekend. Your mom would always feed us breakfast."

They both said in unison, "Blueberry pancakes."

Billy licked his lips. "I must have eaten hundreds of those over the years."

Other guests joined them as the conversation turned nostalgic. "Remember when your dad took us to see *Shrek 2*?" Judy said to Martha.

"Wow, that's not sensitive at all," Betty Jean interjected.

Judy bit her lip. "I'm sorry."

"It's fine," Martha said. "I'd rather focus on the good memories."

"Like making pizza after the movie?" Billy said.

"The kitchen was a disaster!" Judy said, laughing.

"That was the only time I played Frisbee with a pizza," Betty Jean added.

"They were so burned, even the pepperoni didn't come off when we threw them," Billy joked.

"Your dad was amazing," Betty Jean said as she grabbed another beer.

"Do you remember the nicknames he gave us?" Mary asked.

"Mine was Graphy," Billy said.

"He called me Marilyn," Betty Jean said, striking a pose. "I looked her up later. She was the bomb."

"He called me 'Princess,'" Mary said proudly.

"And he called me 'Bubbles,'" Judy said. "He said I had bubbly cheeks."

Martha and Mary exchanged incredulous looks.

"He called you *Bubbles*?" Martha asked.

"Yes! It wasn't a big deal. He had nicknames for everyone," Judy said.

"Remember our trip to King's Kingdom Amusement Park?" Betty Jean said.

"Those lunch meat sandwiches tasted so good after a whole day on the rides," Billy added.

They talked and laughed for hours, but Martha didn't mention the appointments on her father's calendar.

As they were getting ready to leave, Billy pulled Martha aside.

"Can I see you again soon?" he asked.

"Yes. When?"

"Tomorrow. Are you free?"

"Sure. Is lunch good for you?"

"Perfect."

Chapter 12

Martha woke at 6:30 a.m., dressed in her running clothes, and hurried to the in-house gym. Running always helped her think. Was her dad meeting with Judy? If so, why? Why had Ron Phillips lied to them? What did Billy want?

She had looked up the Bistro on Broadway after Billy had called. It was far more upscale than the all-you-can-eat buffets she usually frequented.

These thoughts swirled in her mind as she ran her usual 5K.

When she arrived at the Dinner Bell, cars filled the parking lot, and customers were already standing in line, waiting to get in. Judy waved at her from the kitchen door, looking frazzled. Her eyes were bloodshot, and she seemed hungover.

"Take a seat anywhere," Judy called out. "I'll be with you as soon as I can."

Judy moved like a machine, darting from table to table, taking orders, refilling coffee cups, and dropping off menus.

"What can I get you?" she asked hurriedly when she reached Martha's table.

"I'll have the fruit plate and coffee with cream. But I really need to talk to you," Martha said.

"It'll have to wait until after the rush," Judy replied, glancing at the packed tables and the line of customers outside.

Martha nibbled at her fruit and sipped her coffee while waiting. When Judy finally sat across from her, she looked exhausted. Her shaggy blonde hair was barely contained by a headband, and her flushed face sparkled with sweat.

"I've been working here for three years, and that was the busiest morning we've ever had. What do you need to talk about?" Judy asked, brushing an escaped strand of hair from her face.

Martha hesitated, sensing Judy's weariness but knowing she needed answers. "At the party last night, you said Dad's nickname for you was Bubbles."

"Ya. So?"

"Were you meeting with my father every week?"

Judy crossed her arms and leaned back, her voice low. "Why are you interrogating me?"

"Interrogating? I'm just asking a simple question."

"It feels like an interrogation," Judy said, defensively.

"Please, just answer the question."

"Yes," Judy snapped. "Marriage counseling. I'm getting married. Is that all?"

"For now," Martha said with a faint smile. "I'm sorry if I upset you."

"Right," Judy muttered as she stood up and walked away.

Martha left the Dinner Bell around 9 a.m., her mind still buzzing with questions. Her GPS informed her that it would take an hour and a half to get to the Bistro on Broadway with the current traffic. Realizing none of her outfits felt appropriate, she stopped by the mall to shop for something suitable.

After trying several options, she settled on baby blue slacks, a light blue top, and a knit vest. She arrived at the Bistro fifteen minutes early and sat in her car, observing the patrons. Most were dressed in formal business attire. Her nerves eased slightly when Billy arrived wearing beige dockers and a golf shirt.

The maître d' greeted Billy warmly. "Mr. Davidson, welcome back. We have your table ready."

As they sat, a server arrived almost immediately.

"It's wonderful to see you again, Mr. Davidson. What can I get for you today?"

Billy ordered a rib-eye steak, medium well, with a baked potato and salad. The server turned to Martha and offered, "Might I suggest our blackened salmon? It pairs wonderfully with our steamed asparagus and signature salad."

"That sounds perfect," Martha agreed.

The food was served on fine china with sterling silver utensils. Even the powder room impressed Martha, with a female attendant offering embroidered towels.

Returning to the table, she found Billy waiting patiently. "I didn't tell you everything on Friday," Billy said.

"What do you mean?"

"I told you how your father inspired me to write, but I didn't mention how close we'd become recently. He became a sounding board for me, someone I could bounce story ideas off."

"That's... surprising," Martha said.

Billy explained how he had discovered his talent for writing during a creative writing course at MIT. They laughed, reminiscing about high school days, water balloon fights at the parsonage, and bike rides through the neighborhood.

"Can I ask you something?" Billy said. "Did you know I had a crush on you in high school?"

"On me?" Martha asked, startled.

"You were my dream girl," he said, sheepishly.

Before Martha could respond, her phone rang. She eagerly answered, grateful for the interruption.

"Is Mary with you?" Ruth's panicked voice asked.

"No, I'm in Columbus, having lunch with Billy Davidson."

"She's gone!"

"What?"

"She went to the gym this morning, but now she's missing. I've tried calling her phone, but she's not answering. She's never without it."

"I'll head back right away."

Billy, hearing the conversation, asked, "What's wrong?"

"My sister is missing," Martha said, her voice trembling.

"I'll see what I can do."

Billy made a few quick calls and ushered her into a waiting helicopter at the Columbus airport.

As they flew toward Brownsville, Martha's phone rang again.

Hoping it was Mary, she answered.

"I warned you to let it go!" a distorted voice snarled before the line went dead.

The phone slipped from Martha's trembling fingers as the color drained from her face.

Chapter 13

Martha trembled, staring at the phone on the ground. Billy moved closer, wrapping his arms around her as she collapsed into his embrace, sobbing uncontrollably. He held her tightly, letting her cry until she regained some composure.

"My phone," she whispered, her voice shaky.

Billy picked it up, handed it back to her, and asked gently, "What happened? What did they say?"

She buried her face into his shoulder, her words muffled by tears.

"The voice said... I was warned."

Billy's expression hardened. "I think it's time we call the police."

He retrieved his own phone and dialed 9-1-1. Minutes later, Detective Malroy and Officer Henderson arrived at the scene.

Billy, still supporting Martha, turned to greet them.

"Who are you, sir?" Malroy asked, taking out his notebook.

"Billy Davidson. I'm a friend of Martha's from high school." "Martha, can you tell us what's going on?" Henderson asked, concern in his voice.

Martha wiped her tear-streaked face and recounted the threatening call she'd received as they disembarked from the helicopter.

Malroy frowned. "Are you sure your sister is missing? Maybe she's just out with friends." His dismissive tone caused Martha to tense.

"She's never without her phone!" Martha insisted, her voice rising.

"If she doesn't turn up by morning, come to the station to file a report," Malroy said nonchalantly, closing his notebook and walking back to his car.

Martha watched him leave, her frustration mounting.

Billy placed a comforting hand on her shoulder. "What do you want to do now?"

"I need to see my mom," Martha replied.

"Let me drive you," Billy offered. "If you're okay with it, I'd like to stick around until we find Mary."

Martha nodded. "I'd really appreciate that."

Billy rented a car, and they drove to Ruth's house. Martha's mother was pacing near the door when they arrived.

"Have you heard anything? Is Mary alright?" Ruth asked, her voice trembling.

Martha hugged her mother. "Tell me again exactly what happened."

Ruth explained that Mary had gone to the *Fit for You* gym that morning but hadn't been seen or heard from since.

"We should check the gym first," Martha decided.

At the gym, they found Mary's car in the parking lot. On the driver's seat was a 3x5 card with the chilling message: *I warned you.*

Martha froze, her blood running cold.

"Don't touch anything," Billy instructed. "The police will need to collect fingerprints."

When the police arrived, Malroy was no longer dismissive.

"Ken, interview everyone who saw her," Malroy ordered. "I want to know her every move, every person she talked to."

Officer Henderson headed to the front desk while Martha and Billy followed.

The interviews revealed that Mary had walked on the track and taken a swim lesson.

"She seemed her usual self," the swim instructor noted.

"What did she do afterward?" Ken asked.

"She likely showered like the others," the instructor replied. "Oh, Mrs. Phillips—the senator's wife—was here with her daughter,

Jacqueline. That was unusual."

Despite thorough questioning, no substantial leads emerged.

Billy drove Martha back to Mary's apartment, where they waited with Ruth.

"Do you mind if I stay the night?" Billy asked hesitantly.

Martha blinked in surprise. "Stay the night? I hope I didn't give the wrong impression—"

"No, not like that. I'll sleep on the couch. I just want to be here in case there's news."

She relaxed. "I'd like that. Thank you."

Billy ordered dinner, and the three spent the night in the kitchen, drinking coffee and anxiously waiting for updates.

At 8:00 a.m., the doorbell rang. Officer Henderson stood there, looking tired but resolute.

"Are you still here?" he asked Billy.

"Yes," Billy replied firmly. "I'm here for Martha."

Ken turned to Martha. "I stayed late interviewing everyone at the gym. One man mentioned seeing a large black SUV with a bearded driver circling the lot as if waiting for someone."

"A bearded man?" Martha repeated.

Ken nodded. "We checked the CCTV footage, but mud obscured the license plates. Nobody recognized the driver. It's another dead end for now."

Martha slumped in her chair, despair creeping in.

An hour later, her phone rang. She snatched it up, hoping for good news.

"We found her," Ken announced.

Martha gasped. "Is she alright?"

"We think so," Ken said cautiously.

"What do you mean *think*?"

"She was found on Brickman Road, wearing only her underwear and a winter coat. She's at the hospital now, being checked out."

"She's alive?" Martha whispered, her knees threatening to give way.

"Yes," Ken confirmed.

Martha repeated the news to Ruth and Billy, relief flooding her voice. Though Mary had been found, a storm of questions and fears lingered.

Chapter 14

Martha felt helpless as she stepped into the hospital room and saw Mary curled up in a fetal position, whimpering softly.

"Mary," Martha whispered.

"Martha, it was terrible," Mary said, trembling.

"How are you, darling? You know we'll get through this," Ruth said, gently placing her hand on Mary's shoulder. Mary flinched at her mother's touch.

Mary said to her sister, "It was the bearded man."

"You think it's the same one who came after me?" Martha asked.

Before Mary could answer, a familiar voice interrupted. "Can you tell me what happened?" Everyone turned toward the door to see Ken Henderson standing in full uniform.

Mary looked at Martha for reassurance, and her sister gave her a nod.

"I finished swimming at the gym and was walking to my car when I felt a hand come around from behind me, across my face," Mary began.

"Did you see anyone?" Ken asked.

"Not at first. I felt something cold across my mouth, and everything went dark."

"I overheard you say it was the bearded man," Ken pressed.

"That was when he let me go. He didn't even try to hide his face," Mary said.

"You think he wanted you to see him?" Ken asked.

"I guess so. He looked straight into my face. I couldn't forget it if I tried."

"Could you work with an artist to describe his appearance?" Ken asked.

"I can do better than that," Mary said, flipping over the hospital menu. On the back was a detailed sketch of the man.

Ken stared at the drawing in amazement.

"Mary's quite the artist," Martha said.

"This is him?" Ken asked.

"That's the same man who ran me off the road. I'd swear it's the same one who showed up in my hospital room that night," Martha added.

"Well, at least we have something to go on now," Ken said, carefully folding the drawing. He hesitated before turning to leave, signaling Martha to follow him into the hallway.

Once alone, Ken said, "I don't know what's really going on, but

Malroy doesn't want to take any of this seriously." He pulled a jump drive from his pocket. "I've copied all the files we have on your father's death. There's something off about this case, but I can't quite put my finger on it."

Martha reached for the jump drive, but Ken tucked it back into his pocket. "I'll need to hang onto this for now. These are official documents. Can we meet later to go over them?"

"Call me. First, I need to take care of Mary," Martha replied.

As Ken walked away, Martha saw the doctor emerge from Mary's room. She approached him hesitantly.

"Doctor, can I ask you a question about Mary?"

"I'm sorry, madam, but I can only discuss her case with her or her immediate family," the doctor replied.

"I'm her twin sister," Martha said. "This question is too delicate to ask in front of her. Was Mary... interfered with? You know, sexually?"

The doctor's expression softened. "We're conducting tests to determine that. If you could help prepare her for the possibility, it would make things easier."

Martha returned to Mary's room, unsure how to broach the subject.

"Billy, could you take Mom for a cup of coffee?" she asked.

"Of course. Ruth, let's go," Billy said, gently guiding Ruth out of the room.

As soon as they left, Mary asked, "What's going on?"

Martha explained the upcoming test. Mary's face crumpled, and tears filled her eyes. "I hadn't even considered that possibility, but I guess I need to know."

Martha stayed with Mary throughout the process. After an eternity, the nurse returned, leaned down, and whispered something to Mary. Relief flooded Mary's face.

"There's nothing to worry about," she said, smiling for the first time all day.

The next morning, Mary was discharged. Martha drove her home. "I'm ready to give this up before someone gets hurt," Martha said.

"Don't," Mary replied. "I want to find out who's responsible."

"After all you've been through?" Martha asked, incredulous.

"Especially after all I've been through. He can't get away with this," Mary said firmly.

Later that day, Ken met them at a diner to discuss the jump drive.

"This has all the files on your father's death—witness statements, photos, interviews," Ken explained.

When their waitress arrived, Ken pocketed the drive. "Do you have a computer and printer we can use?" he asked.

"We can use the ones in my father's study," Martha replied. The determination in her voice mirrored her sister's resolve—they weren't giving up until they uncovered the truth.

Chapter 15

They arrived at Pastor Thomas's study shortly after six.

"So, you're here?" Ken said, meeting Billy face-to-face.

"Mary and Martha asked me to come," Billy replied.

"The more, the merrier, I guess," Ken said unconvincingly.

They all gathered around the computer. Ken inserted the jump drive, and the first file appeared on the screen.

"This will take too long. There are over a hundred pages here," Martha said.

"Is there a way to speed this up?"

"We could print all the files and divide them among us," Billy suggested.

"These are official documents," Ken cautioned. "I'm not sure that's a good idea if they ever get out."

"None of us will say anything about it," Mary assured him.

"If they stay here in this office, and we destroy them afterward," Martha added.

"Agreed," Ken said.

Martha hit the print button, and the HP printer hummed to life, spitting page after page of documents. Each person took a stack to read.

"What the heck are we looking for?" Mary asked.

"Anything that seems off," Ken said.

Martha picked up a witness report from her mother. She skimmed through it, searching for anything unusual, though she wasn't sure what that might be.

After about ten minutes, Billy spoke up. "Who's DJ?"

"DJ?" Ken asked. "What do you mean?"

"Jamal's statement says he was with DJ at the time of the murder," Billy explained.

"DJ, who?" Mary asked.

"DJ Richards, his cousin," Billy clarified.

"Have you ever heard Malroy mention a DJ Richards?" Martha asked Ken.

"No, Malroy hasn't let us anywhere near this investigation. But I don't recall that name ever coming up," Ken replied.

"This report says DJ lives in Columbus," Billy said.

"Do you think the police will try to find him?" Mary asked.

"Malroy has no plans to find anyone else. The investigation is over for him, and Jamal is guilty," Ken said.

"If Malroy won't find him, we have to," Martha said. "Jamal's life depends on it."

"What else could Malroy have overlooked?" Mary wondered aloud as she sifted through another file.

Once they finished reading, they shredded all the documents. Then, they went to the Dinner Bell to discuss their findings.

Judy approached their table. "What'll you have?"

"Coffee, hot and black," Billy said.

"I'll have coffee with cream," Martha said.

"Diet Coke for me," Mary added. "Gotta watch my figure."

Martha marveled at her sister's strength. Just hours ago, Mary had been in a hospital bed, unsure of her future.

"So, where do we start?" Martha asked.

"DJ's name could be a game-changer," Billy said.

"Don't get your hopes up," Ken warned. "Malroy is a thorough officer. If he didn't follow up, there's probably a reason."

"Yeah, like railroading Jamal," Mary muttered.

"But why?" Martha asked.

Judy returned with their drinks. "What are you all talking about?"

"We're investigating Dad's murder," Mary said with a smile.

"Didn't the police already do that?" Judy asked, glancing at Ken.

"This is unofficial—just friends tossing around 'what ifs,'" Ken explained.

"Well, I'm not busy right now. I'll play along," Judy said, pulling up a chair.

"What if Jamal is innocent?" Martha posed.

"What if the sun doesn't rise tomorrow?" Judy quipped. "Okay, what if he is innocent? Who else could have done it?"

"That's what we're trying to figure out. You go to church. Did anyone there hate our dad?"

"Hate him? No. Dislike him? Sure," Judy said.

"Who?" Martha pressed.

"Brother Martin, for one. He was head of trustees when your dad nixed the new building campaign. Martin had already hired an architect with his own money and lined up a construction company, thinking the project was a done deal. When your dad said no, he blew a fuse."

"No one would kill over that, would they?" Martha asked.

"Martin supposedly lost $50,000 on that deal and much respect in his professional circle. He stormed out of that meeting, punched a hole in the wall, and left the church entirely," Judy said.

"That's serious anger. People have killed for less," Ken observed.

"Then there's Sister Lewis," Judy said.

Mary laughed. "Sister Lewis? The harmless old gossip?"

"She might seem harmless, but she's got a mean streak. She blamed your dad for canceling the Christmas Bazaar. That event was her pride and joy a few years ago."

"The Christmas Bazaar, really?" Martha said.

"Lewis had been in charge of the bazaar for forty years. When it got canceled, she swore revenge. She was livid—her face turned crimson, and she threatened to 'make him pay.'"

Ken chimed in. "Sister Lewis isn't as harmless as she looks. Last year, she fired a shotgun at her neighbor for stepping onto her property to retrieve his dog."

Billy shook his head. "Wow, I've been safer staying out of church.

This place sounds dangerous."

"No, it's just that churches are made up of people, and people are flawed," Mary said.

"Exactly. It looks squeaky clean from the outside, but on the inside…" Martha trailed off.

"Was there anyone else?" Martha asked Judy.

"Not that I can think of, but those two had the biggest issues with your dad," Judy said.

A young couple with two kids entered the diner, and Judy excused herself to serve them.

"How do we find DJ?" Martha asked the group.

"Maybe you could visit Jamal and ask where DJ lives," Billy suggested.

Ken shook his head. "Malroy will know something's up. He gets a report every time you visit Jamal."

Martha froze. "He gets a report? Is that how the bearded man knows my every move?

Chapter 16

Ken arrived at the office at 7:00 sharp. He was always early. He came through the door to the break room. "Is the coffee ready?"

"Would y'all like a cup? I was just going to refill mine," Candy said.

Candy had worked as a receptionist for the last three years and was itching to enter the field. Malroy has blocked her attempts at every turn.

"This is not women's work," he often said behind her back.

It is unfair to keep an officer with her skills and enthusiasm on the sidelines. She would make a great asset to the force. If he was in charge, she would be out there.

She poked her head around the corner. "Cream or sugar?" She asked. "Normally, yes, but I think I better go with black today."

She set the cups down on the table, smiling, "You know what they say, 'Once you go black, you always go back.'"

"Not a problem."

"What are y'all working on?"

You can take the girl out of Alabama, but you can't take Alabama out of the girl. Malroy, with a red face, hands balled into a fist, and shaking, threw the door open so hard it banged into the wall.

"Hen-der-son!" He yelled.

Ken whispered, "I think I am being summoned."

"Good luck," Candy whispered.

"Yes, sir."

"My office, now!"

Malroy slammed the office door. "What the hell do you think you're doing?"

"Doing?"

"Why the hell are you sniffing around the Thompson's case?"

"Sniffing?"

"Yes, the tech boys have my computer set up, so if anybody opens one of my files, I get an email."

"I think I know what this is about, but if you look, I opened all our files for the last two months."

"All my files?"

"It's a project I'm working on with the chief. You know I love working with computers. I am working on a program to let officers take down all the information while in the field."

Malroy sat down at his desk. "What for?" He asked.

"The idea would be an officer could open their smart phone and fill out the forms right at the crime scene or accident."

"What is wrong with the way we do it now?"

"Now, we fill out our paperwork after we return to the station, and we have to trust our memory and the notes taken at the scene. With this new system, an officer will interview a subject, record this interview digitally, and attach it to a file that would then upload to the cloud."

"Digital, I should have guessed."

Opening the door to the office, Ken turned to leave. "If you have any questions, bring them up with the chief. This is her project. Now, may I finish my coffee?" He asked.

"Her project, I should have guessed."

Ken breathed a sigh of relief as he left the office. He hoped that satisfied him. Malroy was unhappy since the council overlooked him for the chief's position and brought in an outsider, a woman.

Ken drove his cruiser to Highway 872 and parked along the side of the road. This was a pleasant spot to watch for traffic coming in and out of the city. Malroy was sure defensive. He wonders what else he doesn't want anyone to see in that file?

He opened his laptop, inserted the jump drive, and read the files individually.

He carefully scanned through Jamal Richard's file. Even though DJ could give Jamal an alibi, Malroy had done nothing to find him.

As he continued to read, he discovered they found Jamal's fingerprints only in the kitchen and in the study, not in the bedroom where the clothing and money had disappeared. That was a huge red flag, and Malroy should have detected it. The next form to come up on the screen was the hardest one to explain. Malroy charged him with breaking and entering. But there were no signs of forced entry anywhere in the house. No one had disturbed the doors or windows.

What is Malroy playing at? He is a good cop. He knows the procedure, and this case is a mess. No one could have overlooked this much, not a seasoned officer. What is his motive?

A jet-black Mustang sped by. Ken looked at the radar, 83 in and 55. He flipped on his lights. Not on my twatch. The speed limit is the law, and the law is for everyone. After the stop, a kid home from college, he keyed in the number for Martha's phone.

Two rings later, she picked up.

"Martha Thomas, how may I help you?"

"Ken here. Can we meet this evening? I have found more anomalies in your father's case."

"What?"

"Can we talk about it this evening? I am at work." "We can meet at the Dinner Bell if you like?" Martha said.

"Six for dinner," Ken said.

Ken moved his car to the other end of town. The same Mustang came speeding back the other way.

Two tickets in one day, can you say suspension? The early dinner crowd was thinning as Martha came through the door.

Judy saw her. "Table for one?" She asked.

"No, there will be two. Ken will join me."

"I see," Judy said, beaming.

"No, nothing like that. We are just going to talk."

Judy, smiling, said, "That is how it started for me. Now look, I'm getting married."

"Coffee, if you don't mind."

Judy turned toward the kitchen, softly singing, "Here comes the bride, here comes the bride…"

Not me, not again. Ken sat down at six on the dot.

"Have you ordered yet? I am starving. I think I could eat a horse." Martha read the menu and looked up, "No, a horse is not on the menu." They both laughed.

"Are your hands trembling, Ken? I felt I was the only one nervous."

After Ken had devoured his steak and half of this baked potato, he asked, "How was your day?"

"Busy, how about yours?"

He told her about the speed demon in the Mustang.

"To change the subject, Malroy is aware I was in his files."

Martha took a sip of her coffee. "How did that go?"

"Not good. He was hot this morning. He accused me of spying on him and his case."

"What did you say?"

"I told him I copied the files for a project I am working on with the Chief."

"Did he believe you?"

"I don't know, but it got him off my back for now."

"Hay, can I ask you a question, Martha?" Judy asked from behind her.

"Sure."

"We have been friends for a long time, right?"

"Since I moved to Brownsville," Martha said.

"Best buds in high school?"

Martha was not sure where this line was going, but it could not be good.

"I was wondering if you would be one of my bridesmaids? I will understand if you say no, but I really would like you to consider it."

"It would be my honor," Martha said.

"Great, I will get you the name of the dress shop for the bridesmaid's dresses. I know some people have ugly dresses, but not me. I chose a peach dress with hoop skirts. You will love it."

Martha could see the title of the book now in the children's section, "Martha the Giant Peach."

After Judy left the table, Ken continued, "I made two major discoveries today. First, Jamal's fingerprints were not in the entire house, they were only in the study and in the kitchen."

Chapter 17

"There was no sign of breaking and entering at your home."

"Could Malroy have missed those?" she asked.

"Not Malroy. Even a rookie would have caught it."

"And that means?" she said.

"Jamal did not break in and steal the money and clothes. He couldn't have, or his prints would have been in the bedroom."

"I see."

"Because there was no break-in, the implication is your father had to know his killer. He opened the door to his murderer."

"That changes things," she said.

Now, other suspects might be Brother Martin and Sister Lewis. He knew both of them. Who else could have done it?

"I think it is time to get everyone back together. We need to chart our course."

"Everyone?"

"Yes, everyone, including Billy," she said.

"If you say so."

After dessert, Judy brought them the bill. Placing a handwritten note in front of Martha, she said, "Here is the number and address of the dress designer. She will wait for your call."

Martha had forgotten about the wedding and the dress.

The group gathered at The Dinner Bell. Martha, Mary, Billy, and Ken sat around a circular booth at the back of the restaurant.

"What will you all have?" Judy asked.

After Judy returned to the kitchen, Martha said, "I think it would help to hear what Ken has discovered. Ken?"

Ken explained the three problems with the investigation. First, the lack of follow-up on DJ. Second, the absence of fingerprints in the bedroom. And third, the fact that there had been no break-in.

"That means Rev. Thomas let his killer in," Billy said slowly.

"He had to trust him or her," Ken said.

"You can see how this information changes things," Martha said.

"What changes things?" Judy asked as she handed out the drinks.

Martha had not noticed her return.

"We were just talking—"

"About Dad's killer," Mary said.

"How exciting. Can I join in?" Judy asked.

Everyone looked at Martha.

"I guess, if you promise not to discuss what we are doing with anyone."

"Sure."

Martha opened her mouth to say something but stopped herself. Could she trust Judy? The rest of the group did not seem to share her concern.

Would Judy keep her mouth shut? She would need to wait and see.

"I just need to clock out. I will be right back," Judy said. "Now, don't talk about anything important until I get back." The conversation continued after Judy returned.

Mary caught Judy up on the facts.

"We need to make a plan," Martha said.

"What kind of plan?" Judy asked.

"First, we need to help Jamal by finding DJ," Ken said.

"Then we should find out about Sister Lewis and Brother Martin," Billy suggested.

"We don't want to ask Jamal—not if Malroy will know about it. Who else can help us find him?" Mary asked.

"We could talk to Sarah. She might have a line on him," Martha said.

"Who is free to go with me to Columbus tomorrow?"

"Not me. Lunch meeting with my editor," Billy said.

"Me neither. J-O-B," said Mary.

Ken coughed. "I'm free. I have sick days on the books, and I feel a cold coming on."

Everyone but Billy laughed. He just turned away from Ken but stared at him over his shoulder. So childish.

Great. I was hoping to spend some time alone with Ken. The trip to Columbus will give us time to talk. I wonder how he really feels about Malroy.

"Ken and I will check on DJ. Who can interview Brother Martin?"

"Me, me, let me," Judy said.

"Billy, can you go with Judy after your meeting with your editor?" Martha asked.

"Yes," Billy said.

"I can check on Sister Lewis after work," Mary said.

"If it is later in the afternoon, I could go with you," Billy said.

"Let's agree to meet back here tomorrow night and give a report to the group," Martha said.

"Oh, do we have a name for our group?" Judy asked.

"We are just searching for the truth," Martha said.

"How about the Truth Seekers?" Billy suggested.

Everyone nodded in agreement, except Ken.

"So, we agree. 'The Truth Seekers' will meet back here tomorrow at six, ready to report," Martha said, closing the meeting.

Martha returned to the motel and took Scruff for a walk.

"Ken and I are going to spend tomorrow together. Great, huh?" she said to the dog as he sniffed around for the right spot. "Hurry, I want to make sure I get plenty of sleep tonight so I can be in top form."

Chapter 18

"Can we take the Camaro?" Ken asked as he stepped from his Chevy.

Throwing the keys to him, Martha said, "So, you want to drive?"

"I always wanted to drive one of these."

"It handles like a dream."

"This is your second one, right?"

"They totaled the first one. Thank God for insurance."

Ken wheeled onto the highway and took it up to 80 mph. "Sweet! This car holds the road and takes curves like a dream."

Martha smiled. "I think you may be in love."

"You may be right," he said, passing a semi.

"There's the sign for Bloomberg. Time to slow her down," Ken said.

"Bloomberg?"

"Yes, they write more speeding citations in this little berg in a month than we do in a year. It's their primary source of income."

Just inside the village limits, a police car sat hidden behind a billboard.

"Can I ask you something?" Ken asked.

"Okay."

"You know I like you, right?"

"I like you too."

"I don't mean like. I mean, I really like you. I think I'm blowing this. Well, I've gone this far. Do you really like me?"

"Ken, you're a great friend, and maybe, after we find out what happened to my father, you'll become more than a friend. But for now, we need to focus on what we're doing here in Columbus. I'll tell you when I'm ready to be more than friends. Is that okay?"

"So, I have a chance?"

"You have more than a chance."

This is awkward. I need to change the subject.

"Have you decided what you're going to do about Malroy?"

"I was hoping to get some advice from you."

"I'm not sure I can advise you on a matter like this, but I can listen." "If Malroy has purposefully misled the DA, and he knows there are witnesses who can prove Jamal is innocent, I'll need to take it to the Chief," Ken said.

"What kind of proof will you need?"

"I hope to get some today. I'll take down DJ's statement. That, along with the other problems with this case, should be enough for the Chief."

"What will happen to Malroy?"

"I don't know."

The car was silent for the rest of the trip.

As they pulled up to Sarah Richards's home, Martha said, "Maybe I should take the lead since she knows me already."

"Smart move."

"Can I get you two something? Water or iced tea?" Sarah asked.

"Iced tea would be nice," Martha said.

"Same for me," Ken said.

Sarah handed them the glasses. "Now, why did you want to see me? You sounded so mysterious on the phone."

"Sarah, have you talked to Jamal lately?"

"He called yesterday. He's out of the hospital and healing. I can't wait for him to get out of that place. It's pure evil."

"That's what Ken and I want to talk to you about—helping him get out."

"How can you do that?"

"If we could find DJ, his cousin, and interview him, it might help your son."

"DJ? I haven't seen him in weeks. He and Jamal would hang out at Balls to You. It's a bar and billiard club on Main Street. That's all I know. I hope it helps."

"When we leave here, we'll see if we can find him."

Sarah took a sip of her tea. "But you two may not want to go down there. It's a pretty rough crowd, and they're all black." They finished their tea and rose to leave.

"Remember what I said about Balls to You. It's not a safe place for you two."

Chapter 19

Ken and Martha drove to the pool hall. The weathered, paint-peeling sign read **"Balls to You."** The letter **B** was formed by two billiard balls stacked on top of each other, with a pool cue on the left-hand side completing the shape.

They parked and headed for the door.

Was that a black Tahoe she just saw parking on the next block? She was probably being too suspicious. There must be hundreds—no, thousands—of black SUVs in Columbus.

Ken walked up to the bartender. "Can you help me out?"

"No."

"We're looking for DJ Richards. Have you seen him?"

"DJ, who? Never heard of him."

"His aunt said he often comes here," Martha said.

"Don't know him, never heard of him, and besides, I'd never help a pig."

"What makes you think I'm a cop?"

"You cops are all alike. You *are* a cop, right?"

"I'm not a police officer. Will you help me?" Martha asked.

The bartender turned away and wiped down the bar. "I don't help pigs or the friends of pigs."

A young, muscular Black man with a pool cue in his right hand walked toward them. "It's okay, Big Dave. If my aunt sent them, they check out."

"Are you DJ?" Martha asked.

"Yes. What's this all about?"

"We want to talk to you about Jamal," Martha said.

"How is he?"

"Not well. They're going to try him for murder," Martha said.

"Murder? I was told that was settled. When I talked to the detective, he said they dropped it."

"What?" Ken asked.

"He said I wouldn't need to testify or anything."

"When did you talk to him?" Ken asked.

"Last week. I called him because I hadn't heard anything, and he said everything had worked out. That's true, right?"

"I'm afraid he lied to you. Jamal is awaiting trial right now," Ken said.

"What a piece of crap. He was gonna let me sit here while they locked my best cousin away for life. What a shit."

"Now that we've found you, maybe we can get this straightened out," Martha said.

"I'll do anything I can."

Ken opened a little black notebook. "Can you tell us about your movements on the afternoon of December 12?"

"Damn, you really *are* a cop."

DJ leaned back in his chair and yelled, "Big Dave, you nailed it. He *is* a cop."

"I can always tell," Big Dave said, smiling.

DJ set his chair down and faced Ken. "Jamal and I went to the hospital to see his mom. She had surgery that day, but she wasn't in the room.

Do you want to know Jamal flirted with the nurse?"

"Tell us everything. It might help Jamal," Martha said.

"Okay. He was doing his thing with this nurse. I don't know her name, but she had big bo—oh, you know."

"Anything else you remember about her, besides her bra size?" Martha asked.

"Sorry. She had long crimson hair. I remember because Jamal joked that she was already on fire for him."

"Did you go anywhere else?" Ken asked.

"Yeah, we went to Hotdog Heaven," DJ said.

"What's that?" Ken asked.

"It's a place that sells hotdogs—the best hotdogs in Columbus. Deepfried hotdogs."

"Did you see anyone while you were there?"

"The girl that waited on us was hitting on both of us. She bent real low when she put our dogs on the table so we could see down her top. She had little to show, but she gave a peek away."

"Do you think she'll remember you?"

DJ pulled out his wallet. "She gave both of us her number."

"Would you be willing to go with us to the hospital to see if we can find that nurse? Her testimony could save Jamal," Martha said.

"Hell, yeah!"

"Big Dave, I'm leaving. Keep the table warm for me." They walked out the door together.

"Do you mind riding in my car? It's the black Camaro," Martha said.

DJ walked around the car. "Damn, girl, that's the real shit. You own it?"

"Rental," she said.

The sound of two shots echoed off the surrounding buildings. DJ crumpled to the ground.

Ken pulled a snub-nosed Smith & Wesson from his ankle holster and took cover behind the car.

A black SUV squealed its tires and sped down the road. Ken fired once, shattering the SUV's back glass. It turned a corner and was gone.

Martha stood over DJ and watched as he bled out. She knew that as the blood drained from his body, the only hope for Jamal was also slipping away.

Ken called 9-1-1. They spent the rest of the afternoon in interviews with the Columbus police and filling out forms. They were told they'd need to return if the gang members were caught.

Martha told Ken, "That was no gang member."

"I know, but they don't seem to believe us," Ken said.

"What else could happen?"

The drive back to Brownsville was silent.

Chapter 20

Martha and Ken arrived back at The Dinner Bell at 5:30. Just as they sat down at a table, Ken's phone rang.

Looking at the screen, Ken said, "I need to take this."

He excused himself and stepped outside, pressing the phone to his ear. A few minutes later, Mary and Billy walked in together.

Judy appeared from the kitchen. "Let me tell them I'm taking my break now."

They all gathered around Martha.

"DJ is dead," she said.

"What?" Billy exclaimed.

"It was horrible. Someone shot him—right there, on the street, in front of us."

"Shot?" Mary repeated in shock.

Judy, just joining them, looked around. "What did I miss?"

"DJ is dead," Mary said. "Martha was just telling us."

"Someone shot him," Billy added.

The table grew silent.

Martha, her hands shaking, took a sip of her tea. "Without DJ, our only hope of helping Jamal is to find the real killer."

"Are you sure he's innocent?" Judy asked. "My mom and dad said—"

"Why else would someone kill DJ, if not to shut him up?" Billy interrupted.

Martha pulled herself together. "We need to find the real killer. So, what did you find out?"

Judy spoke first. "Old Brother Martin is rude. When we told him we wanted to talk about Jerry Thomas, he yelled at us to get off his porch and out of his yard. Billy tried to reason with him, but he just screamed a bunch of awful things about your dad before slamming the door in our faces. I told my mom how mean he was—"

"Did you tell her anything else?"

"I might have… My mom and sister always ask about my day. I'm sorry. I won't do it again. I forgot about my promise."

Martha frowned. She feared she couldn't trust Judy. This was proof. From now on, she'd have to be careful about what she shared with her.

"Okay, but no more leaks. What about Sister Lewis?"

"She was funny," Billy said. "I'm trying to work our conversation into my next book."

Martha turned toward Billy. "Funny how?"

"She was as pleasant as could be. Invited us in, offered us sweet Southern iced tea— 'made the right way.' Then she asked why we were there. Billy said, 'We'd like to talk to you about the day Rev. Thomas died.'" Judy nudged Billy. "Tell them exactly what she said."

Martha cringed at Judy's phrasing.

To tell them, not to carefully and exactly tell them, she thought.

But she forced herself to set aside her mental grammar book and listen.

Billy continued. "She looked at me with this giant smile and said, 'So I'm a suspect? How exciting.' Then she turned to me and said, 'Someone told me you girls were becoming detectives—like ScoobyDoo. Do you have your own Mystery Machine?'"

Judy added, "Then she left the room and came back with a double barrel shotgun. She asked, 'Would you like to look at it, maybe smell it, like they do on TV, to see if I've fired it?'"

Billy nodded. "I asked her, 'Do you have any handguns?' 'Darn, I don't own one of those. All I have is Old Betsy here,' she said."

Billy chuckled. "Then she invited us to the backyard to watch her shoot it. I said yes. It was a hoot, watching that enormous woman load and fire a 12-gauge. She's not a bad shot." Everyone at the table laughed.

Ken returned and sat down. "What have we gotten ourselves into?"

"The phone call?" Martha asked.

"It was the police in Columbus. They found the SUV with the broken back window."

"And?" Martha pressed.

"Someone wiped it down, but they were able to lift a print from the seat adjuster."

"So, we can find out who was driving?" Billy asked.

"Yes and no."

"Yes, and no?" Martha frowned. "Either we can or we can't."

'I *abhor* that answer,' she thought.

"They identified him," Ken said. "But here's the catch—he was reported dead in Iraq over ten years ago." Silence fell over the group.

Finally, Mary asked, "Dead how?"

"According to Army Special Forces, he died in Iraq when an IED blew up the truck he was driving," Ken explained.

"How is that possible? He was in Columbus today," Martha said.

"I think he might be a spook—CIA or something. Maybe they faked his death."

The table went quiet again.

After a long pause, Martha asked, "So what do we do now?"

"I don't know about them, but *you* and *I* are going back to Columbus," Ken said. "We have an appointment with the chief of detectives Monday at 10:00. Believe me, they're taking this seriously now."

"While we're there, let's find the nurse and the other girl," Martha said.

"Nurse and other girl?" Billy asked.

"There's a nurse at a Columbus hospital who can prove Jamal wasn't here the afternoon of Dad's murder. And some girl from a hot-dog stand who can alibi him too."

"What are their names?" Judy asked.

"I have the hot-dog girl's number, but we only have a description of the nurse," Ken said.

Judy frowned. "How do you plan to find a nurse in Columbus based on a description? What do you know about her?"

"We know where she works. She has long red hair and is… well, *blessed*," Ken said, glancing around the table.

"Blessed?" Judy raised an eyebrow.

"She has big breasts," Martha said flatly.

Judy sighed. "Great. You're looking for a hot, redheaded nurse with big tits. Sounds more like a porno video."

Everyone chuckled softly.

Martha was sure everyone was wondering the same thing Ken had earlier: *What have we gotten ourselves into?*

Ken and Martha arrived at the Columbus Police Station at 9:45. The duty sergeant led them into the office of Detective Bedale.

"Tell me everything, start at the very beginning," Bedale said.

Martha told him about her father's murder.

"Wait a moment," Bedale said as he checked a file. "I thought I remembered reading that a thief took a Tahoe from the long-term parking lot the same day as the murder. Please go on."

Ken then explained Martha's accident, Mary's abduction, and what happened to DJ. He also pointed out everything Malroy had missed in his investigation.

Bedale leaned back in his chair. "I hate to piss on your bonfire, but Malroy is a complete A-hole and does not understand police procedure."

"Unfortunately, that is not the case," Ken said.

"Then he is bent."

"That is my fear, which is sad because he has always seemed a model officer," Ken said.

"That's the way it always is. No one suspects anything until it comes out. I had a partner who was bad, but I don't know," Bedale said.

They both got quiet, and the only sound Martha could hear was the office noises outside the door.

After what felt like an eternity to her, Bedale spoke. "We need to keep Malroy out of the loop, just in case."

"I agree," Ken said.

"Now, what are you going to do?" Bedale asked.

"We are going to find the nurse and the girl from the hot dog place," Martha said.

"I wish I could assign an officer to help, but we are down two men because of budget cuts," Bedale said.

"I think we will be okay. I am carrying," Ken said.

"What about you, Ms.?" Bedale asked.

"What about me?"

"Are you also carrying?"

"No, I have never… No. I never needed to."

"I believe you may have the need now, if you don't mind me saying so."

"What a great idea," Ken said. "I wish I had thought of it."

I never thought of myself as a pistol-packing mama, but it might not be a bad idea. Someone might try to kill me again. I might even want to suggest it to Mary. No, Mary with a gun is a scary thought.

"If what you said is true, you are dealing with a killer who has already killed twice. One more will not worry him," Bedale said.

"Or her," Martha added.

"Do you have any suspects?"

"Just the bearded man," Ken said.

"Harley Frank," Bedale said. "That is his name, for what good it will do you."

"We are on our way to the hospital to find the nurse," Martha said.

"I am going to see what I can find out about this Harley Frank," Bedale said. "Call me and let me know what you find out."

"Will do, and you call us if you learn anything," Ken said.

Bedale led them to the door. "Ms., think seriously about what I said about the firearm."

They drove to Greater Columbus Hospital. Greater Columbus was an older hospital, but they kept it well maintained—fresh paint on the walls and colored lines on the floors to help you navigate: yellow for surgery, red for the ER, blue for patients' rooms. They rode the elevator to the eleventh floor, the floor Martha had received from Sarah.

When the elevator doors opened, they saw into the nurse's station. It was easy to pick out the nurse from DJ's description. She was 5'10, with long red hair, and the other part of his description was also true— at least a D-cup. She wore a uniform designed to "Let the boys out to breathe." Martha looked over at Ken. His eyes were as enormous as saucers—a boy in a candy store.

She tapped him on the shoulder. "Really?"

He shook his head slightly and followed her out of the metal box.

"May we speak to you?" Martha said to the nurse.

The nurse turned toward Martha. "Sure thing."

Martha pointed to a waiting area. "Over here, maybe?"

"One sec," the nurse said. She turned and said something to the other nurses in the cubicle.

When she walked out from behind the counter, it became clear she liked to display what God had given her. Her uniform was somewhere between a micro-mini and something decent, and much closer to the micro-mini.

She walked over, and her eyes locked on Ken's. She sat down in an overstuffed chair. "What can I do for you, sweets?"

"We would like to ask you about a young man who was here to visit his mother a few weeks ago," Martha said.

"I see. We have tons of people going through here. I am not sure I can remember one person, but I will try," the nurse said.

Ken took out his phone. "Do you mind if I record this?"

"Sure, record away."

"First, what is your name?" Ken said.

"Trista, Trista Johnson. That is T-R-I-S-T-A. Do you need my address and phone number?" she said, winking at Ken, who smiled back.

"I think all we need is your name for now," Martha said.

"Do you have a picture or anything?" Trista asked.

Martha pulled up the picture Sarah had sent her the night before.

"Sure, I remember him. He came to see his mother. She had surgery. He and his friend could not see her. She was out of the room."

"You are sure it was him?" Ken asked.

"Yes, he was smoking hot. I tried to get a date with him."

"Do you remember what day and time you saw him?" Ken asked.

"Let me check my phone. Here it is—Wednesday, December 12, at 1:30. I took a picture of him and his friend."

"Thank you, I believe that is all we need for now," Martha said.

"Sure, you don't need my number or address?" Trista asked Ken.

Martha stood up. "This will be fine."

Ken said, "Yes, give us your contact information in case we need to contact you later."

Martha glared at him.

After Martha and Ken were back in the elevator, Martha said, "Did you get an eyeful?"

"Eyeful?"

"Don't tell me you were not looking at her."

"It is only polite to look at someone who is speaking to you."

"But you don't have to drool."

"I did not drool."

"Well, don't be so polite to the hot-dog girl."

The drive over to Hot Dog Heaven was silent. They sat in the car and called the number Ken had.

"Hello, Kali here."

"Hello, my name is Ken Henderson. I am a police officer and would like to talk to you. Are you at work now?"

"Yes, what is this about?"

"I will be there in a moment. We can discuss it then."

He hung up his phone. "She is there."

They both came in and saw a teenager with her father waiting.

Ken approached them. "May I talk to you for a moment, Kali?"

"You the police?" her father asked.

"Yes."

"Can I see your badge?" Ken flashed his badge. "You no talk to my daughter. You go now."

"I just need a moment of her time. If I leave, I will be back with men in uniforms, and that will disrupt your customers. There is no need for that."

"You talk for just a minute."

"Yes, and you can stay here."

He looked at his daughter. "You talk."

"I want to record this. I can send you a copy," Ken said to the father.

"She talks now."

Martha dug her phone out of her purse and showed her Jamal's picture. "Do you remember seeing this man here on December 12 in the afternoon?"

***

Kali looked at her father, who nodded his head yes. "He was here with a friend."

"You flirted with him?" her father asked.

"No, Papa."

Ken stood up. "Can you show me how you make deep-fried hot dogs? I have never heard of such a thing."

Kali's father agreed and left the table with Ken. Her father walked toward the kitchen, gesturing animatedly.

"We are alone now, Kali. You need to tell me the truth."

"I did flirt with them, but I was too young for them, I think."

"You are sure they were here?"

"I gave them both my number, and I don't do that a lot."

"Thank you for the honesty."

"I think we will have two of those deep-fried hot dogs," Ken said as he returned to the table with Kali's father.

"Kali, you put in the order. These are on the house," Kali's father said.

Back in the Camaro, Ken said, "Two and a half hours."

"What?"

"It took us two and a half hours to prove that Jamal could not have murdered your father."

"Yes," Martha said. "So?"

"Malroy was going to let that poor boy spend the rest of his life in prison over two and a half hours of work."

"That does not look good for Malroy."

"I think he is bent, like Bedale said," Ken said. "What a waste."

"What now?" Martha asked.

"I guess I take what I have to the Chief. I now have the proof."

"Do you want me to go with you for support?"

"That would be great," Ken said. "I will need all the support I can get."

Ken turned the car off the highway.

"Where are we going?" Martha asked.

"A surprise."

They pulled into the "Bare Arms Gun Shop and Range."

"Are you serious?" Martha asked.

"As a heart attack."

"I am game."

Customers crowded around, looking at handguns in glass cases, various targets, and accessories for different long guns and handguns.

"Do you have a range open?"

"Rifle or handgun?" the attendant asked.

"Handgun."

"This way."

The teenage boy led them to the range, had them read the range rules, and then handed them ear and eye protection. "Range rules."

Ken ushered Martha to the firing line, removed his S&W .38 from his holster, and placed it on the shooting stand. He then explained to Martha how to hold, aim, and fire it.

"Would you like to try it?" Ken said, pushing the button for the remote target to move back twenty feet.

"Sure."

"Now, remember, expect a kick when you pull the trigger. It's not like on TV—it will really jump."

Martha picked up the pistol, aimed, and fired three quick rounds, cleared the firearm, and placed it back on the shooting stand.

Ken's mouth dropped open as he pushed the button to retrieve the target. There were two holes in the heart and one in the center of the forehead.

Martha shrugged her shoulders. "It pulls a little to the left, but a nice little pistol."

"Why did you not tell me you could shoot?" Ken asked.

"You never asked. What do you think there is to do in Texas? I go shooting with my friends every weekend."

"You are an excellent shot." "

I prefer my Glock at home."

"Thus ends the lesson," Ken said.

After they arrived at Martha's motel, Ken opened the glove compartment of his car and removed a Ruger LCP nine-millimeter. "I would feel more comfortable if you were carrying."

"No, I will not let them scare me into carrying a gun."

"Please, reconsider."

"I will think about it."

"I guess that will have to do."

Chapter 21

Ken and Martha arrived at The Dinner Bell at 6:00 p.m. They drove around the parking lot three times until they found an open spot and pulled in. At the front door, they found two couples waiting to be seated, one with children.

When the rest of their party showed up, Martha said, "I don't think this is a good place for our discussion."

"I agree. There may be some nosy parkers around here," Billy said.

"Where can we go?" Mary said.

"We could go to our home," Martha said.

They arrived at their home and spread out in the front room. Martha and Ken brought them up to speed on what had happened in Columbus.

Thank God he didn't mention going to the gun range.

"So now we know Jamal is innocent," Billy said.

Mary came from the kitchen with canned soft drinks. "So where does that leave us?"

"We need to pursue the leads we have," Ken said.

Martha looked at Ken and said, "We also need to find out who Malroy is involved with and why. I will get some paper from Dad's study so we can take notes."

Martha opened the study door and made a wide berth around the bloodstain.

She looked on the desk for a notepad and could not find one. Opening a drawer on the left-hand side of the desk, she pulled out a notepad, and a silver Cross pen rolled out of the pad. She picked it up and returned to the group.

Martha sat down, notepad and pen in hand. "Here we are. What should we do next?"

"We need to speak again to Brother Martin," Judy said.

Mary took a sip of her soda. "Martha and I can check on him."

Martha looked up. "Yes, Mary and I will check on him."

"Has anyone performed a full forensic search of your father's computer?" Billy asked.

"The police have not," Ken answered.

"Should we do that?" Martha asked.

"Yes, it could give us more information," Billy said. "Can we put this on the list?"

"I agree," Mary said.

"Can I go look at it now?" Billy asked.

Martha wrote on the corner of the pad, tore it off, and handed it to Billy.

"Username and password." Billy disappeared into the study.

He came back ten minutes later. "I am going to need some time to do this. Can I borrow a house key for a few days? Your dad had awesome Reds stuff. Are those jerseys real?"

"Right down to the signatures," Martha said.

Ken and Billy went to the office. After they returned, Martha read from her notes, "Tomorrow, Mary and I will visit Brother Martin."

"Take a helmet with you. You may need it," Judy said.

"I will see what I can do with the computer," Billy said.

Ken looked up. "I will see what I can find out about Malroy."

Martha looked at Judy. "Can you make a complete list of everyone who had problems with my dad?"

"If Martin did not do it, then who did?" Martha asked the group.

After the group broke up, Ken and Martha were alone.

"You know someone is going to need to check on Rick Phillips," Martha said.

"I know, but let's not tell Judy, at least not yet," Ken said. "Would you like to get a cup of coffee?"

"Sure, we could go to The Dinner Bell."

When they arrived at The Dinner Bell, the parking lot was almost empty. They parked in front.

"What can I get for you two?" the server asked.

"Coffee for me," Ken said.

"Caffeine-free coffee for me," Martha said.

"Tell me about yourself," Ken said.

"Me? There is not much to tell."

"Humor me."

"I grew up in a United Methodist pastor's home, so we moved frequently. We have lived in Marystown, Columbus, and then we moved here."

"What made you want to work in a library?"

"My love of books."

"I never was much of a reader."

"Reading is the greatest way to learn and grow. There is no subject you cannot become an expert in if you read enough."

"Really?"

"If you read and study for one hour a day on any subject for ten years, you will be an expert in that field."

"You could become an expert investigator," Ken said.

"If I had ten years."

They parked in the motel's lot.

Ken escorted her to the door. "May I ask for a kiss on the cheek?"

"Not brave enough to go for the lips?"

He took her face softly in his hands and kissed her lightly on the lips.

She opened the door, looked back, and winked. "That was nice."

Martha came through the door to find Scruff waiting for his nighttime walk.

"Scruff, it was great. He kissed me. I know I told you I don't need a man in my life, but it might be nice."

Scruff took his evening walk while Martha kept talking about Ken.

Billy and Martha met at the Thomases' house. Billy began by turning on the computer.

He moved through the files. "Was your father a computer expert?"

Martha laughed. "Mom said she saw a computer like his first one at the Smithsonian Museum when they visited Washington, D.C. He has had one ever since I can remember. Why?"

"He has created a hidden partition that is password-protected."

"What is a partition?"

"He has set aside a part of the hard drive so it does not show up with a normal search."

"Can you open it?"

Billy's fingers sped over the keys of the keyboard. Line after line of numbers and letters appeared on the screen.

"Damn," Billy said.

Again, he entered the code and pressed enter.

"This is not working," Billy said.

"Is it important?" Martha asked.

"It could be."

"So, what do you need to do?"

"I will need to have people who know more than I do to look at it."

Billy punched a number into his phone. "Billy here. I need you to crack a code for me on an HP desktop."

Then he listened for a moment. "I can link you in if the internet has enough bandwidth."

Martha glanced at her smartwatch. "I need to meet Mary. We are going over to see Brother Martin."

"I will stay here and work on this."

"I will be back as soon as possible."

"Martha, do you mind if I make a ghost of your father's hard drive?"

"A ghost?"

"An exact duplicate of the hard drive."

"Yes, whatever."

Chapter 22

Mary and Martha turned into the Martins' driveway, past the ten-foot pillars that stood sentry at the entrance to the property. The massive home was behind an eight-foot-high stone wall. The front yard was an acre of perfectly manicured grass, even now in January. Who mows in the winter?

Martha recalled her father saying, "Brother Martin thinks he is richer than God."

As they followed the driveway, they passed an outside pool, larger than the one at the motel, buttoned up for the winter months.

Martha parked by a new BMW. They rang the doorbell, and a young housekeeper answered the door.

"How may I help you?"

"We would like to see Mr. Martin," Martha said.

The housekeeper led them into a mega-sized front room with Masonic items on the wall.

"Martha, Mary, it is so good to see you. Come in and sit down. Tell me, how is your mother doing? I miss seeing her. How are things at the church? Would you like a piece of apple pie? The cook just made one," Sister Martin said.

Brother Martin stood in the doorway. "Don't bother. They will not be staying that long."

Sister Martin crept back to her chair. "I am sorry, dear, I did not see you come in."

"My sources tell me you fancy yourselves as Nancy Drews, so what do you want?"

"We would like to ask you about the day our father died," Martha said.

"Will no one rid me of this meddlesome priest?" he said.

"Dear, he was a Methodist minister, not a priest," his wife said.

His eyes narrowed, and he glared at his wife.

"What questions do you have?"

"First, where were you on the day he died?" Martha asked.

"Why should I answer any of your questions? You are not the police." Martha stared into his eyes. Bluff—bullies collapse when confronted.

"The police could follow us," she said.

He laughed. "Not this police force. They know which side their bread is buttered on and who supplies the butter."

He opened his smartphone and checked his calendar. "Not that I need to explain myself, but I was visiting a lodge in Lancaster, and there are twenty Masonic brothers willing to testify to that fact."

"Now this is done and dusted. Would you like that piece of pie?" his wife asked.

"I said no!" he shouted.

"Just curious. Why did you come to me?" he asked.

"We heard about your argument with Dad," Mary said.

"Oh, he may be your father, but because he was pig-headed, I lost a lot of money and some influential friends. Your dad was a real asshole."

"Herbert Mortimer! There is no call for that kind of language," his wife said.

He turned and stormed out of the room.

"Girls, I apologize for his behavior. His temper was the reason we left the church. He swore he would never forgive your father as long as he had breath," his wife said.

"It is not your fault," Mary said.

"Despite his outburst, it was great to see you both again."

"Maybe we could meet sometime without him," Martha suggested.

His wife led them to the door. "I could never do that."

As they drove away, Mary said, "He was wrong, you know. Dad was not a priest."

Martha looked at her and giggled, but not wanting to explain England's history, she said, "I know."

But the question Martha was asking herself was, did he hate her father enough to kill him or hire someone to do it? Maybe he hired the bearded man.

"I need to go home and take Mom to the store. She also asked for you to come to church tomorrow," Mary said.

Martha dropped Mary at the apartment and drove back to the house to make sure she had locked everything up. She pulled to a stop outside the house and saw that Billy's car was still there.

She opened the door. "Now who is a workaholic?"

Walking through the front room, she opened the door to the study.

Someone had scattered files on the floor, and filing cabinet drawers were all open.

"Billy!"

He was lying on the floor in a pool of blood. There was a gash in the back of his head. He was motionless.

She rushed to his side. "Billy, wake up, Billy!"

Nothing. No movement, no sound. Billy just lay there.

"Billy!"

Slowly, he opened his eyes. "What happened?"

"I don't know. I found you just lying here," she said.

"I remember seeing a man with a beard pouncing, then everything went dark," Billy said.

She helped him to his feet. Wrapping her arm around his waist, she started walking him toward the front door. He stumbled and fell into the front room. She struggled to get him back on his feet. They got into the front yard when Billy collapsed on the browning grass. The blood seeping from his head tinted the grass crimson.

She pulled her phone from her jeans pocket and dialed 911.

As she hung up, she heard a whoosh. She looked up from Billy's prone body and froze. She could see a fire spreading through her father's study.

Tears traced their way down her face as she watched the fire grow and consume the front room.

In moments, the fire engulfed the entire wooden structure. She felt helpless as the flames took from her the front room where she had celebrated Christmas. Her father had taken her senior pictures on that staircase. The blaze consumed her bedroom, where she wrote in her journal. Her life was going up in smoke before her eyes.

She stood and watched as flames licked up the outside wall. Fire was consuming the house like a famished bear devouring its prey. The heat and smoke pushed her away, the smoke stinging her eyes and taking her breath away. Yet the house pulled her in.

The police arrived and called for an ambulance and the fire department. By the time the fire trucks arrived, all they could do was make sure the fire did not spread to other homes. Her home was a total loss.

Billy was unconscious. They rushed him to the hospital. She followed the ambulance.

After breakfast in the hospital's café, Martha rode the elevator to Billy's floor. She opened his room's door and saw Betty Jean sitting by his bedside, holding his hand.

Betty Jean walked to her. Martha put out her arms to hug her. Instead, Betty drew back her hand, swung it hard, and hit Martha in the face.

"You and your obsession almost cost him his life."

The pain spread across her face, and the shock set in. Martha, embarrassed, turned around and headed for the elevator. She returned to her car, sat there, and burst into tears. She started the car and just drove. After a half hour of driving, she was sitting in front of the remains of her family home.

Smoke was rising from the ashes. Black and gray charred remains were all that remained. The firefighters were putting out flare-ups. Investigators were working their way through the mess.

Her mind went back to all the memories she had made in that home.

The fire department finished up, packed their truck, and left the site. She got out of her car and picked her way through the debris. She was stepping over the pieces of her life—not just her life, but the lives of her father, her mother, and her sister. She walked through what remained of her father's study. His files were ashes. The computer was a blackened shell.

Maybe Betty Jean was right; it had become an obsession. Look at all the people she had hurt. They kidnapped Mary, DJ is dead, and now Billy may die. It is not worth it. With the evidence they now have, they will free Jamal. What more can she do? Leave it to the police. They are trained for this kind of investigation. They will find out who the guilty parties are. She is finished. She would put no one else in danger.

Her phone rang. "Hello."

"Martha, are you okay?" Mary asked.

Had she heard about the fire, or had she heard about Billy?

"I am okay, but I need to talk to you and Mom."

"Have you heard about Billy? He is in the hospital."

"I know, I was there," Martha said.

"You were? Where was that?"

"At our home."

"Oh. If you are near there, could you stop by and pick up Mom's green dress?"

"I need to talk to you both. I will be over to your apartment in a few minutes."

What will she say to her mother and sister? How could she explain what happened to their home and to Billy?

She drove to her sister's apartment.

Ruth and Mary were waiting for her.

"I don't know what you have heard," Martha said.

"We heard Billy is in the hospital. That is all we know. How is he?" Mary said.

"He is unconscious."

"What happened?" Ruth said.

"The bearded man attacked him at our home," Martha said.

"In our home?" Ruth said.

"Yes, and I need to tell you something," Martha said.

Just then Ruth's phone rang, and she looked at the screen. "I need to take this."

"What!" she said.

Ruth punched the button to hang up. Her face turned red, and her hand clenched into a fist.

"What happened to the house?" she demanded.

"That is what I came to talk to you about—"

"Get on with it. Rumor is our house burned to the ground," Ruth said.

"The rumor is true," Martha said.

"It had something to do with this quest of yours, I'll bet."

"Mom, I am so sorry. I never planned for this to get so out of hand."

Ruth's face whitened. She stumbled into a kitchen chair. "Is it all gone?"

"I am afraid so."

"What am I going to do? What are we going to do?"

"You have insurance, right?" Martha said.

Ruth moved toward the sofa and lay down. "Insurance? Insurance can't replace memories. A lifetime of memories, pictures, gifts, keepsakes—up in smoke."

Martha felt terrible already. This was just aggravating her despair.

"I better go," Martha said.

"You know how Mom is," Mary said.

She knew how their mother was, and this time she was right. There was no bringing back what she had lost.

She returned to the motel and dropped onto the bed, weeping.

This is going nowhere. I was threatened. Mary was kidnapped. The house was burned, and now Billy may die.

"Scruff, I cannot keep going. I am putting my family and friends at risk. Had I not arrived when I did, Billy would be dead. He would have been in the burning house. The cost is too great."

Tomorrow, she thought, *I will tell everyone it is over. Let the police do their jobs.*

Chapter 23

Martha pulled her car off the highway into the parking lot of the Dinner Bell. It was nearly empty except for a yellow Jeep and a black SUV.

She pulled open the door and looked around, breathing a sigh of relief. No bearded man. There were a couple of teenagers, a boy and a girl, looking into each other's eyes and laughing. A young family now filled the booth Martha and her crew normally occupied.

The dad was busy helping his toddler daughter complete a connect-the dots picture on the back of the menu with a pencil. The woman was struggling with an infant, his face covered with mashed potatoes that had migrated into his blond hair, his arms waving wildly, all the while testing his lungs. She looked up to see Martha staring at them.

"He missed his nap," she said, her face turning red.

Martha walked past them and toward a booth on the other end of the building. "You have beautiful children."

"Thank you."

The father looked up and smiled.

Several groups came into the restaurant. Would there be too many for them to talk?

Martha watched the family drama unfold as the mother fought to clean up the screaming child with a wet napkin. The child was winning.

What kind of mother would I be at thirty years old? It might be time to find out.

By the time the family left, Judy and Mary were coming through the front door. They looked at their normal spot, then looked around until they saw Martha in a different booth. Mary shrugged his shoulders and walked toward his sister.

As they sat down, a server lost her grip on one of the large silver serving trays, and meatloaf, mashed potatoes, and beef stew all came crashing to the floor. Martha looked at it and thought it resembled a piece of modern art.

"She's new," said Judy.

A man in a white shirt and black pants, wearing a silver badge with the word "Manager" imprinted on it, came flying through the double swinging doors from the kitchen.

"What happened?" he said.

Judy ran over and helped with the cleanup. The manager returned to the kitchen and came back a few moments later with a mop and a bucket. Together, they cleaned. Ken came through the front door, started toward the booth, and gave a wide berth to the mess in the middle of the floor.

"What happened here?"

"It happens," Judy said, looking up from the floor.

What a team they have, working together for a common goal.

After the cleanup, Judy came back to the booth, the rattled server following her.

The waitress stopped at the edge of the table. Trembling, she asked, "What can I get you?"

"Take a breath, it will be okay. I will have a Diet Pepsi," Judy said.

The rest gave their orders, and she walked toward the double doors to the kitchen. She looked at the mess. It reminded her of this entire investigation.

Ken spoke first. "Malroy is up to something."

"What?" Mary asked.

"I don't know, but he is out doing interviews and building a fresh case. It's like he knows they will never convict Jamal," he said.

"Who is he going after?" Martha asked.

"I have no clue," he said.

"Maybe this is a helpful development," Martha said.

"What do you mean?" Judy asked.

"We are in over our heads," Martha said. "We need to leave it to the police."

"Can we trust them? Sorry, Ken, but..." Mary said.

"I understand. I feel the same way," Ken said.

"Why are we giving up?" Mary said.

"Think about it, Mary. They kidnapped you. Ken, your boss is angry with you. And poor Billy is in the hospital," Martha said.

"Billy is in and out right now. I went to see him today, and during a lucid moment, he asked to see you, Martha," Judy said.

"You need to go see him, no matter what Betty Jean wants," Mary said.

"I will tomorrow," Martha said, but she was not excited about seeing Betty again.

Ken sipped his tea. "Is there anything we can do to find your father's murderer? It just feels unfinished to me."

"Me too, but we are out of leads. We have pursued everyone. Besides, the house is gone, Dad's files are gone, and his computer is gone," Martha said.

"What about Brother Martin?" Judy asked.

"He was in Lancaster, like he said," Martha said.

They agreed they had done all they could. They finished their drinks and went home.

Martha felt relief but also guilt. What would her father say about dropping it? She could hear him say, "If you start something, don't give it up."

Martha dropped into bed after taking Scruff for a walk.

"What a mess, Scruff, and there is nothing I can do about it."

Chapter 24

Martha woke the next morning, showered, and ran a 5K on the treadmill in the in-house gym.

Then she drove over to visit her mother and sister.

Mary opened the door and ran her fingers through her hair. "What time is it?"

Martha stepped inside. "Almost eight o'clock."

"Shit, woman, don't you ever sleep in?"

"I will put some coffee on. Do you want a cup?" Martha said.

"I'll grab a cup with ya in a minute."

Mary headed to the back of the apartment while Martha headed for the kitchen.

She found the coffee in the cabinet next to the refrigerator and put a pod in the Keurig. As she waited for the coffee to brew, she flipped on the television. Some news show was on. The reporter was talking about how Jeff Bezos became the second man alive worth over one hundred billion dollars. *What she could do with that kind of money.*

She would return to the job she hated in San Antonio.

"Coffee ready?" Mary asked from behind her.

"Almost. Do you want regular or a special blend?"

"I see you use that new fancy one you bought, not the old Mr. Coffee."

"Why would I buy it if we will not use it?"

"Okay, a cup of the chocolate coffee would be good this morning. Might wake me up."

"I see you finally came to your senses," Ruth said from the doorway to the front room.

Martha looked up from her cup of coffee. "What do you mean?"

"What I mean is, have you dropped your foolish investigation?"

"We have stopped, at least for now."

"I told you it would come to no good."

They were silent for a few minutes. Then there came a knock on the door.

Mary walked toward the door. "Who could that be?"

She opened the front door with Ruth and Martha standing behind her.

"May we come in?" Malroy asked.

Mary opened the door, and Malroy and Henderson came in together.

"Has there been a development?" Martha asked.

Malroy walked toward Ruth. "You might say so."

He stopped directly in front of Ruth, pulled a card from his shirt pocket, and read, "Ruth Thomas, I am arresting you for the murder of your husband, Jerry Thomas. You have the right to remain silent. If you give up—"

"What the hell is going on?" Mary asked.

"Do your job," Malroy said to Henderson.

Henderson walked to Mary. "Mary Thomas, I am arresting you for conspiracy to commit murder—"

"Ken?" Martha whispered in disbelief.

"It is my job, nothing personal."

"Seems damn personal to me," Mary said.

Malroy smiled while he put the handcuffs on Ruth and finished his speech.

Ken was not smiling, but he cuffed Mary and led them both down to the cruiser, placing them in the back seat.

Before Ruth got in, she turned to Martha. "I told you this would end badly."

"Is that a confession?" Malroy asked.

"No, just an excited utterance," Martha said. "Now she is going to keep silent, aren't you?"

Malroy stared at Martha. She had learned about excited utterances from his book—*thank you, Malroy.*

Ruth nodded her head.

"I will get a lawyer for you both this afternoon," Martha promised as Ken helped Ruth into the seat beside her daughter.

Martha waved at her mother and sister as they disappeared in the cruiser. Then she just stood there. The car was gone. Her mother was gone. Her sister was gone. She could not move. Was I the cause of this? She felt the heat of tears as they streamed down her face.

She glanced at her Fitbit and noticed an hour had passed since the police left with Ruth and Mary.

She felt something rubbing her legs. She looked down to see Scruff walking circles around her legs.

"What are we going to do now, boy?"

Her first task was to contact a lawyer. She took out her phone.

"Hey, Siri, give me the number of a criminal lawyer near here."

"I found Spital, Spital, and, Bits Attorneys at law, would you like that one."

"Yes."

An hour later, she was face to face with Farrell Spital, the senior partner of the firm.

He leaned forward, placed his arms on the desk, and stared at her, "Your name is?"

Martha also leaned toward him, "Martha Thomas."

"Thomas? Are you related to Jerry?"

"Did you know my father?"

"I have eaten lunch with him every Wednesday the last several years. We are in the Rotary club together. How is Ruth doing with all this?"

"That is the reason I am here. The police arrested her and my twin sister Mary this morning for my dad's murder."

"Ruth, she would hurt no one."

"Tell that to Detective Malroy."

"Daniel, he arrested her."

"You know him," Martha said as her heart sank.

"Rotary Club as well."

"You need to talk to Daniel," Martha said.

Spiral Pulled a legal pad from a desk drawer, "No, I need to talk to DA Furgeson. Would you mind if I step out for a few minutes and make a phone call?"

"No."

He left Martha alone in the large office. Unable to sit any longer, she walked over and examined the plaques of the wall.

He earned his doctorate in Jurisprudence from Harvard. There were two framed copies of the Harvard Law Review with Articles by

Farrell Spital, one Martha wanted to read, "Mitigating Cultural Bias in the Courtroom." Then there were many pictures of him with various Republican political figures, including one shaking hand with the former President, George Bush.

However, in the center, in the place of prominent was an 8x10 of Farrel enjoying a meal with the late Justice Clarence Thomas. He came back 15 minutes later, "Furgy, I mean DA Furgeson feels he has 'a slam dunk case against both your mother and sister.' I don't know if it is hubris or confidence, but I fear the latter."

"Why?"

"He is going to the grand jury day after tomorrow. He did not get to be the DA by rushing ahead with weak cases. Furgeson said it was mostly circumstantial—"

"But you wrote an article about circumstantial evidence."

"Yes, I said circumstantial evidence is not always reliable and it needs interpretation, but several people are on death row because of circumstantial evidence."

"What can we do?"

"First, I need to become Ruth and Mary's Attorney of Record, pay me $100, sign the forms, and then I can represent them."

"Just a hundred dollars. I heard these kinds of cases can cost hundreds of thousand even into the millions."

"This is going to be a pro-bono case, Jerry helped me through a painful divorce, this is the least I can do for him."

He picked up his phone, pushed a button.

"Cindy, can you bring a client package for Ms. Thomas, she has just hired us to represent her mother and sister."

"Do you think I can get in to see my mom and sister?"

"If they are being charged with murder, I would not be surprised if they permit no visitors," he said, "is there something you want me to ask? I know I can get in."

"Just let them know I love them and check to see how they are doing?"

"Okay, and I will call you later today to let you know what I have discovered."

"So, I have done all I can do?"

"Yes."

Martha stayed in the car, fearful about going in to see Billy, especially after what happened with Betty Jean. She rode up in the elevator. The doors opened, and Martha stood there, looking both left and right to see whether she could spot Betty Jean in the hallway. She crept toward Billy's room and slowly opened the door.

Then, behind her, she heard, "Martha? Martha, is that you?"

Martha turned around and saw Betty Jean coming toward her fast. It was too late to run. She pulled her arms tight into her body, her heart racing.

She wasn't sure what to expect. She closed her eyes tightly, fearing the next thing she would experience would be a stinging cheek.

Betty Jean wrapped her arms around her, pulled her in close, and whispered in her ear, "I'm so sorry. I overreacted. Can you ever forgive me?"

Betty Jean and Martha went together into Billy's room. He was waking up.

"How are you, Martha?" Billy said.

"I'm doing well, but what about you? How are you doing?"

"The doctor said I'm doing well, and I should be getting out of here in the next twenty-four hours."

Martha looked over at Betty Jean, who said, "That's what we're expecting. He should be home by tomorrow."

Billy looked up at them, his eyes half-closed. "Do you mind if I go ahead and get some sleep? I'm exhausted. The nurse gave me something to help me sleep."

His eyes closed, and he began to snore softly.

Betty Jean and Martha slipped out of the room. Martha said, "How about I buy you a cup of coffee?"

Betty Jean said, "That would be wonderful."

They went down to the cafeteria and settled in at one of the tables. Doctors and nurses sat around them, lost in conversation.

"How is Billy really doing?" Martha asked.

Betty Jean responded, "He's doing as well as can be expected. The doctor said he took quite a hit, but he seems to be coming around well. How are you doing? I've heard about what happened to your mother and sister."

"Well, I'm doing as well as I can. You heard that Ken arrested them? How could he do such a thing to my family?"

Betty Jean looked at her and said, "Remember, he may have just been doing his job. It may not be anything personal. Give him the benefit of the doubt."

"I don't know if I can."

"He really likes you. Everyone sees it. I think I'm going back to

Billy's room. Consider what I said."

She decided she owed it to Ken to at least listen to his explanation.

Farrell called and said he needed to see her.

Chapter 25

Farrel was waiting for her in the empty law office. The office, which had seemed alive just hours ago, was now dark and cold. He led her through the dim hallway to his office, which was brightly lit.

He pulled a paper from the top drawer of his desk and handed it to her. "We may have a problem. I just received the incomplete witness list from the DA. Do you recognize any of the names on this list?"

She read over the names and addresses. "I know the first one, Mrs. Watson. She's lived next to us since we moved here."

"What about the others?"

"I don't know this Mr. Boday, but he lives on the same street as Sarah Richards."

"Who is Sarah Richards?"

"She's the woman my father had an affair with."

Farrel grabbed a legal pad and pen. "Holy shit. You better tell me everything—start from the beginning."

Martha told Farrel the whole, tangled story.

"Damn. That complicates things," he muttered. "We need to find out what these people told the police. I hate surprises when I get to court."

"Surprises?"

"Yes. Like when I find out I've been lied to, or when someone only tells me part of the story. Thank you for being honest with me. That is the whole story, right?"

"Honestly, that's all I know."

"We could go talk to Mrs. Watson now if you have time," he suggested.

"Won't your wife be waiting for you for dinner?"

"I'll call her. She loves Jerry and Ruth—she'll understand."

After a quick two-minute call to his wife, and another to Mrs. Watson to check if she was home, they were on their way.

Mrs. Watson answered the door on the first ring. "Let me look at you, dear. You've grown up! I haven't seen you since you went off to university."

"Hi, Mrs. Watson. This is Mr. Spital, and we have a few questions for you."

"Sure, come right in. Would you like a cup of tea? Maybe a biscuit?"

"Biscuit?" Farrel asked.

"A cookie," Martha clarified.

"That would be lovely," Martha said to Mrs. Watson.

After serving them tea and cookies, they settled into the front room. "I heard you were in the hospital," Mrs. Watson asked.

"It was nothing," Martha replied.

"About our questions," Farrel interjected.

"Don't get your knickers in a twist," Mrs. Watson chided. "I just need to catch up with one of my girls first."

"Mrs. Watson, can you tell us what you told the police?" Martha asked.

"Oh, that nice Bobby who came by? I told him how I've lived next to your mum and dad for years, and I never once heard them row. Oh, they had the occasional squabble, but nothing serious. But two days before your dad died…"

"What happened two days before?" Martha prompted.

"It started as a squabble, you know, but then it turned into a full-on barney. And then, two days later—Bob's your uncle—he was dead."

"Could you hear what they were arguing about?"

"Oh, yes, dear, they were so loud I couldn't help but hear. Your dad said, 'It's over.' And your mum shouted back, 'I will kill you and your b-i-t-c-h too.' Of course, she didn't spell it out. I'm sorry, dear, but that's the truth."

"Thank you, Mrs. Watson. We needed to know," Martha said, her voice steady despite the shock.

"You poor dear. I wish I could have told you something else, but you asked for the truth."

"It's okay. You told the truth—that's all you can do."

Farrel turned on the car. "That is bad."

"I know. What do we do next?"

"We need to know what Mr. Boday has to say. I'm in court for the next three days. Could you talk to him? It would be best to take someone with you as a witness in case we need it later."

"I'll find someone and go tomorrow."

"I'll go home and write up this interview for the record, but I hope this never gets into the courtroom. It could go south."

He drove her back to the office. She picked up her car and drove back to the motel.

As she pulled into the lot, she saw Ken waiting for her.

"What do you want?" she asked.

"I didn't know."

"What didn't you know? That they were investigating my mother and sister for murder? Or that you were going to arrest them?"

"I didn't know any of it."

"So, you just showed up at the house, and he said, 'Let's arrest someone today—how about Ruth and Mary?' Right?"

"Let me explain."

Martha paused, remembering Mary Jean's words: *…he may not have known it was coming.*

"Okay."

"Malroy came up to me at the station and asked me to serve a warrant with him. We do this all the time. I didn't know it was for your mother or sister until we pulled up in front of your house. He looked at me, smiled, and said, 'Let's go do our job.'"

"That was it? The first time you heard about it?"

"Yes. He opened his car door and walked up the stairs. Before we knocked, he said, 'I will arrest Ruth for murder. You will arrest Mary for conspiracy to commit murder.' Then he knocked. And the rest… well, you know. I'm so sorry, Martha."

"So am I. But I can't blame you. You were just doing your job."

"If there's anything I can do…"

"Are you free tomorrow?"

Ken pulled into the motel parking lot at exactly 7:30 a.m. Martha was waiting for him, her Camaro running. As he climbed out of his car, she motioned toward the driver's seat. He slid behind the wheel. Pulling out of the lot, Ken asked, "Want to stop for coffee?"

They drove through the Golden Arches, picked up coffee, and got back on the road.

"How are things at work?" Martha asked.

"Tense."

"Why?"

"I turned in the information on Malroy to the chief."

"Wow. What happened to him?"

"Nothing yet, but the chief told me it's just a matter of time."

"She agrees something's wrong?"

"She's doing her own investigation."

"How long will that take?"

"I don't know, but Malroy has been treating me differently since I copied his files."

"Do you think he knows you reported him?"

"He might."

"What could he do?"

"There's no telling."

They drove in silence for the rest of the trip.

"What address are we looking for?" Ken asked.

Martha consulted the paper Farrel had given her. "2800 Overcourt Drive."

They pulled to a stop in front of Charles Boday's house. From where she sat, Martha could see into Sarah Richards's front yard, directly across the street.

Martha and Ken walked to the front porch and rang the doorbell. She noticed a video doorbell system. She pressed the button, and a few seconds later, a voice came through:

"Be there in just a sec."

A moment later, Charles Boday opened the door. He looked to be in his mid-forties, anything but fit or trim, with a beer belly, fleshy face, and balding head.

"You must be the folks from Brownsville?"

"My name is Martha Thomas, and this is my friend Ken Henderson."

"Can I get you something to drink? A soda pop, maybe a beer?"

"We're just fine, Mr. Boday. We had coffee on the way up," Ken said.

"Well then, let's get right down to business," Charles said.

"Can you please tell us what you told the Brownsville police?" Martha asked.

"Well, sweetie, it was more about what I *showed* them than what I said. I bet you'd like to see it too." "If you don't mind," Martha said.

"Don't mind at all—seeing's free." He tapped a few keys on his keyboard, and suddenly, a massive 96inch screen lit up. At first, it was just a view of Sarah Richards's house. Then, a car pulled up in front of it. Martha's heart sank. It was her sister's car. Her sister was driving. Her mother sat in the passenger seat.

"If you'll notice the date and time stamp, this was the same day your daddy died," Charles said. "But the best part is coming up."

Martha watched as her mother got out of the car, walked over to the vehicle parked in Sarah's driveway, and dragged a key across its paint.

The final shot on the enormous screen zoomed in on the car door. Scratched into the blue paint were the words:

DIE BITCH.

"She was short on words, but I think she got her point across," Charles said.

"Would it be possible for us to get a copy of this video?" Ken asked.

"Sure enough. I can send it to your email—for $100."

"$100?"

"Broadband up here is mighty expensive. Big town and all. Of course, you could just wait until you see it again in court."

"Will you take a check?" Ken asked.

"Cash is so much friendlier."

Martha dug through her purse and pulled out four twenties. Ken added another twenty from his wallet. They handed the cash to Charles.

"See? Nice and friendly."

Ken gave him his personal email address. Martha and Ken waited in the car until the video arrived as an attachment.

They drove to Burger Boss and ordered lunch.

Martha pulled out her phone and searched for "Charles Boday." Their meals arrived on blue plastic trays—burgers piled high with lettuce, tomatoes, and onions, with home fries on the side.

"Thank you for visiting Burger Boss, where *you* are the boss," the server said before walking away.

"Here's something interesting," Martha said. "Phillip's campaign recently hired Boday as a consultant."

"Consultant?" Ken raised an eyebrow.

Martha swallowed a bite of her burger. "This is even more interesting. Up until last year, he worked on an oil rig in the Gulf of

Mexico."

"So, what kind of consultant is an oil rigger?"

Ken stared at his phone. "Something's not right about this video."

Martha adjusted her seat to see his screen better. "I know. I can hardly believe my mother would do such a thing."

"No, I mean something's *wrong* with the video itself. But I can't put my finger on it."

Martha's phone vibrated on the table. She picked it up—Billy was calling.

"Martha, I need to see you as soon as possible. I think I've found something," Billy said.

"Ken and I are in Columbus, but we'll be back in town this evening. Can we meet at the Dinner Bell at five?"

"Five would be great. I have a phone conference with my publisher, but it should be over by then."

She hung up and told Ken about the conversation.

"So, we're meeting him at five," Ken muttered, rolling his eyes.

Was that resentment or jealousy she saw in his expression?

Chapter 26

Billy was waiting at the Dinner Bell at 5:00 when they arrived. They parked right in front of the main door.

Billy met them at the entrance, "Have you had a busy day?"

"Don't ask," Martha said.

Billy held the door open, "That bad?"

"Yes," Ken said, "We could use some good news."

Judy yelling from the kitchen door, "Our booth is open."

Billy wiggled into a booth, "I may have some."

Judy came over, brushing her strands of hair from her brow, pulling her order pad from her apron, "What will ya' all have."

She was still full from the Burger Boss meal, "Just coffee with cream for me."

"I want a steak, medium rare, with a salad, and loaded baked potato." Ken said.

Billy studied the menu, "Cob salad with a glass of water with lemon."

Ken looked up, "Could I get green beans on the side?"

Where does he put it all?

Martha leaned forward in her seat, "What did you find out?"

Billy sat forward, "I was looking at the ghost—"

Ken's eyebrows raised, "Ghost?"

"An exact copy of my dad's computer."

"Yes, as I looked at the copy, I discovered a hidden partition on his hard drive."

"What is a partition?" Ken asked.

"It is a way to divide a hard drive into multiple hard drives," Billy said.

"So, how does that help us?" Martha asked.

"You father put something he did not want anyone else to see in a partition. It looks like it contains audio files from your father's study," Billy said.

Ken leaned forward on his elbows, "He recorded his office?"

"Everything," Billy said.

"The murder?" Ken asked, a smile on his face.

"Here it is," Billy said, pulling a flash drive across the table.

Ken tapped the drive, "We might have the killer's voice right here."

"I can't tell you. When I heard the gunshots, I turned recording off. There may be voices, but I did not hear any," Billy said.

"Did you find anything else?" Martha asked.

"Did you?" Judy said holding everyone's order on a silver platter.

"Not yet, but there are hundreds if not thousands of files to go through," Billy answered.

Judy handed out the food. Ken and Martha showed them the video from Boday.

Shaking her head, Judy said, "That is bad."

Martha looked at her, "We know."

Billy watched it a second time, "There is something off."

"I thought so too, but I could not put my finger on it," Ken said.

"I am going to see if I can get in to see my mother and sister and see what they have to say," Martha said.

The conversation changed to the upcoming game. Thank God. Martha was not sure she could talk anymore about murder, her mother, her sister.

She returned to the motel and took Scruff for a walk, and then dropped into bed, no reading, no television, her mind could not absorb any more today.

***

Martha woke and went down to the gym.

Great, no one else is here yet. Now where is the remote for the television. She picked it up from the table below the T.V. mounted on the wall. Turned it on and walked to the nearest treadmill and walked and watch.

5k will be good for this morning, she thought, as she programmed the machine.

A game show she had never heard of was on the screen. The contestants were trying to guess answers to historical questions.

Not bad, I could get about half of them right.

Then the screen changed, a banner announced a News Alert. Next on was a very sober-looking reporter in a suit and tie standing in front of Billy's home.

He lifted his microphone and said, "This morning the world lost a great literary mind. During a home invasion, they struck the author Billy Davidson down in the prime of life. Many of his readers, however, know him as William David. He has authored several New Times best sellers…"

She stopped listening and just stood there. Could it be true, it has to be. It was just on the news. She looked in the mirror. How did she get back in her room, what time was it? An hour had passed since she heard about Billy.

She showered and dressed. "I need to find Ken, he will know what to do. Where would he be, he might be at Billy's home?"

She drove to Billy's home and discovered police cars, state police, local police, and news trucks all over the front yard. A young police officer was trying, without success, to hold back the flood of reporters from breaking through the crime tape barrier.

She picked up her phone and dialed Ken's number.

"Martha, I cannot talk. They have murdered Billy."

"I know, I am in my car outside."

"Wait right there, no one is being allowed in, but I will come out to you as soon as I can," the phone went dead.

Her phone rang a few minutes later, "Ken?"

"No, Ms. Thomas, this is Farrel Spital's secretary called to set an appointment for you to meet with him this afternoon. What time would be good for you?"

"I just lost a very dear friend. I don't think I can meet today."

"I am sorry to hear that, perhaps you can call the office tomorrow, he is eager to see you, Ms. Thomas. So, until tomorrow. I am sorry about your friend," the phone went dead.

Something else I will have to deal with. How will I tell him about the video? Her mind replayed the video. Both Billy and Ken saw something wrong in it, but what.

There was a tap on her window, Ken stared in at her, "Let me in."

Ken opened the door and slid into the passenger's seat, "It is confusion in there."

"What happened?"

Ken turned toward her, "We think Billy interrupted a robbery when he came home yesterday from dinner."

"With us?"

"He came in and someone shot him."

"Why?"

"He had thousands of dollars wrapped up in televisions, recording equipment, and computers. According to his maid, she found him, he had one room filled with computers, monitors, and printers. It looks like he had his own server from the racks that are left."

"Left?"

"Everything is gone. They took their time. They have taken everything worth anything."

Poor Billy, he came home to this.

"Wait a minute, what about the ghost?"

"Everything is gone," Ken repeated, solemnly.

***

Martha needed to see her mother and sister, and the best person to help her was Farrell Spittal.

Martha drove to his office.

The secretary looked up from her desk, "May I help you?"

"I was hoping to see Farrell Spittal for a few minutes."

"Who may I ask is calling?"

"Martha Thomas."

"I am sure he will want to see you. Please have a seat."

Martha had just set down when she said, "He will see you now."

Martha took the overstuffed leather-covered chair in front of

Farrell's desk, "Sir—"

He held up his first finger as a way of saying wait a minute. He studied closely the paper in front of him. Pushing the paper away from him, sliding his glasses down his nose, and looking over the lenses, Farrell asked, "What did you learn from Boday?"

Martha's stomach jumped. The mention of his name reminded her of the video.

"He has a video," she mumbled.

"Of what?"

"Here, I will let you see for yourself."

Martha pulled out her cell phone and flipped to the video Ken had sent her.

Martha started the video playing, her hands were shaking, she breathed faster, and she stepped back a step from the desk.

"Are you okay, Ms. Thomas?"

She moved back another step, "I am fine!"

"You don't look fine. Would you like a glass of water or something?"

"No, I will just take a seat."

He took the phone from her and propped it up on his desk and leaned it against an open book. He watched in silence. Then he slid the selector back and began it again. Martha came around the desk and watched it with him.

After the second viewing, he opened his desk drawer and pulled out a Sherlock Holmes pipe and a pouch of tobacco, "Terrible habit, but it helps me think, do you mind?"

She walked back to her chair shaking her head no, "This is bad, right?"

He packed the tobacco into his pipe, lit it, drew the smoke into his lungs, released it slowly, in smoke rings. His body went limp, and he just waited.

He took another draw on the pipe, followed by silence. And then another, more silence.

Was he about to drop the case, what would she do? This was really damaging. Finally, he spoke, "This is harmful. I can see the D.A. after he plays it for the jury, he will have a large blowup of your mother's face looking right at the camera."

"That is true. She looked right at the camera, like she knew it was there," Martha said, "But there is something else wrong with it. Can you play it again?"

This time Martha watched it closely. She was trying to ignore the fact it was her mother and sister on the screen, "There is something wrong, but I cannot put my finger on it."

The color was returning to Farrel's face, "Would a larger screen help?"

"Yes, it might."

"I don't know all the tech stuff, but my secretary is a master at that kind of thing."

Martha rubbed the back of her neck. Someone else would now see the video.

"If she can help, but she also has to keep it confidential, right?"

"Yes, but don't kid yourself. Once this trial starts, this video will get out, it will go, what do they call it, virus."

"Viral, you mean it will go viral."

Farrel pushed a button on his phone, "Can you step in here and help us out."

"Viral, I was afraid of that," Martha said under her breath.

The door opened, the secretary stepped in. In a few minutes she had the video up and ready to play on the 55-inch large screen TV in his office.

The secretary walked toward the door, "If that is all you needed, I have some invoices I need to send out."

Thank God she will not see the video, at least not now. Martha seeing her mother larger than life, doing unmotherly actions.

Her stomach churned.

Focus, she needed to focus.

"There, did you see it?"

"See what?" Farrel stammered, studying the screen.

"The hedges, that is wrong."

"Hedges?" he said.

"Yes, someone trimmed the hedges."

Farrel slumped back in his chair, "So someone trimmed the hedges."

"But they were not trimmed."

"What?"

"When my sister and I went to visit, Sarah had not mowed the grass or trimmed the hedges. That was just a few days after the murder. Hedges don't grow that fast."

Farrel picked up his phone and searched through his Rolodex "It won't help us in court, but it gives me an idea."

He found the card he was looking for and dialed, "Chuck, Farrel Spittel, I have a video I need you to look at. I need to know if it is real or not."

He listened for a moment, "Just like the divorce case last year with the fake video."

Holding the phone to his ear, he listened again, "I will have it sent over right away, make this a rush job, okay."

Farrel hung up and turned toward Martha, "Last year, we had a wife who brought a video to court that showed her husband with another woman. After we studied the video, we discovered it there was no other woman. She had a friend put the woman's face over hers in the video. No promises, but that might be what is happening here."

"A fake," Martha said.

"Right, and the judge was angry, I have never seen him snap at anyone like he did her and her lawyer."

"So, it may not be real?"

"Let us not worry about the video for now, it is what it is. We have a bigger problem."

Martha felt her heart racing, and her knees weaken. She had to set down before she fell. She could not take any more bad news.

"The fire inspector found the gun that killed your father in the ashes of your home. Do you have any idea how it got there?"

"A gun, my father and mother don't have a gun."

"They found it in the remains of your home, and the ballistics match the bullets used to kill your father."

"I need to see mom, I have to ask her about this and the video, can you get me in to see her and my sister?"

Martha arrived at the local jail at ten o'clock the next morning. They escorted her into a small room divided in two by a long metal table. At the half point of the table, a Plexiglas shield reached the length of the room. She sat down in the metal chair provided. A green steel door opened on the far wall away from her, and her sister and mother entered dressed in orange jumpsuits.

"Martie, it is so good to see you," Mary said.

"How is it going for you?" Martha asked.

"Terrible, this is a real hellhole. Can you get us out of here?"

"I am working on it."

"What is the delay? It is ridiculous to think I would have shot Jerry," Ruth said.

"I have some questions for you two. Did you and dad have a fight over Sarah Richards?"

Ruth stood up, now angry, "What does that bitch have to do with anything?"

Martha tapped her fingers of the metal table.

I need to remain calm, but she is not making it easy.

"Mrs. Watson, your neighbor, said she overheard you and dad fighting. I just need to know if that is true," Martha said.

"He had a child with that bitch, did you know that? Your perfect father had an affair."

"We need to know about the fight."

"Yes, hell, yes, we fought. He had lied to me and given her and her son money for all these years. Money that was rightfully mine, ah, I mean ours."

"They have asked her to testify in court."

"All couples fight."

Martha rubbed the back of her neck, "Well, this question is for both of you. Did you drive to Sarah Richards' home?"

"No!" Mary said, "The first time I was there was with you."

Ruth turned away from Martha, "I don't know where she lives, and I don't want to know where she lives. I hope I never see her again."

"Why do you ask?" Mary said.

"There is a video that looks like you two at Sarah's house the day of the murder."

"Like hell. I have never been there," Mary said.

Ruth turned back and raised her eyebrows, "Video, how?"

Martha's head was now throbbing, "I am just telling you that I have seen it."

Mary stood up and slammed her fist into the table, "I promise you Martie it is not me or mom. We were shopping before the murder."

Martha tugged at her blouse, "Let's forget about the video for now."

"Sounds good to me," said Mary.

"Any other bad news, daughter?"

Martha was sweating now.

I don't want to ask them about the gun, but I need to. Martha turned to face Ruth and said, "Did you and dad own a gun?"

"Gun, are you crazy! You know how I feel about guns. I will not have them in the house."

"Why are you asking about a gun?" Mary asked.

Martha fidgeted in her chair, "They said they found a handgun in the remains of the house. It is the same gun used to kill dad."

Ruth slumped back in her chair, "Someone has really set us up. They know about the argument, they created a video, and now they have a gun. We don't have a pray, do we?"

"Don't give up, I am working on this."

"Nothing against you, dear, but you are out there and we are in here. Based on what you just told me, I would convict us. I think it is over," Ruth said.

Martha stood up and leaned into the Plexiglas screen, "You can't think like that, we will find the facts. Ken, Judy, and I will not stop looking until we have uncovered the truth."

"That is easy for you to say, you are out there, we are in here dressed in our fashionable orange," Mary said.

"Your time is up." The officer said from the door.

"I will be back soon, keep the faith," Martha said.

Ruth and Mary shuffled out the door, and Martha left the room. Martha returned to her car. Her face was warm, and she felt tears form in her eyes and running a path down her cheeks. She sat there and cried.

Was mom right? Is there no hope left?

Chapter 27

Martha's phone vibrated. She pulled it out and punched the green icon.

"Martha Thomas, how can I help you?"

"Hello, Ms. Thomas. This is Farrel Spittal's secretary. He understands you have had a major loss; however, there are recent developments in your mother and sister's case."

Martha glanced at her watch. "What time would be good for him?"

"He said sooner is better. He has an opening at 1:00 if he can get the others here."

"Others?"

"I will put you down for 1:00."

The phone went dead.

Others? Who else could possibly be at this meeting? She would find out in an hour. But who could it be?

Martha grabbed lunch on her way to Spittal's office and arrived at a quarter to one.

She waited outside in her car until one, then made her way to the office.

"They are waiting for you. Go right in," the secretary said.

There were three men waiting inside—Farrell, a man in his fifties wearing an expensive suit, but the other man was something else. He had bright red hair down his back with a matching-colored beard, cut-off jeans, and a black t-shirt that read, "Mead, it's not just for Vikings anymore."

Farrel walked toward her. "Let me introduce you to everyone. This is the DA, Furgeson."

Martha shook her head slowly. "I am no legal expert, but isn't he the last person who should meet with my mother and sister's lawyer? No offense."

"I am confused also," Furgeson said.

"I will explain everything, just wait a second," Farrel said.

"I'm waiting," Martha said.

"Me too," Furgeson said.

"This is our video expert, Chuck. He has been working for Hollywood for years. Anytime we have a questionable video, we contact him."

"Questionable?" Furgeson asked.

Chuck stepped over to a 55-inch digital television. "Let me explain."

He pushed the play button, and the video of her mother and sister filled the screen.

Martha told herself, *Calm down, it is just a video.* Then she looked over at Furgeson, who was smiling like a child who had just won first prize at a county fair.

"On first view, this looks like a car carrying Subject A and Subject B."

"Looks like?" Furgeson asked.

"Yes," Chuck said. "Looks like, but I will show you what is really happening."

He once again picked up the remote and pushed a button. The video fast-forwarded to the section where her mother was at Sarah's car. Then her mother faced right at the camera.

"Here. This is what I want you to watch closely."

He pushed a button on his laptop that connected it to the television. His laptop screen was now on the television screen.

"I took this video apart, slide by slide, and though it was a professional job, they made some mistakes. In this slide, when Subject A looks at the camera, you will notice when we enlarge that slide, there is a slight mismatch between her face and the rest of her head. It is only off by one-half a degree, but it was enough to tell me there was a problem."

"Problem?" asked Furgeson. "It looks good to me."

"Can I continue?"

"Please do," Furgeson said.

"Once I discovered this problem, I looked for other anomalies. That is when I asked for high-resolution photos of Subject B's automobile."

Farrel turned to Martha. "We had an investigator go to your sister's home and take several photos for him to use."

"I see," Martha said.

"I again enlarged the slides on the video that I felt had the clearest image of the car. Then I noticed a crease in the back fender well.

Both vehicles have the crease, but Subject B's real car—"

Martha faced Chuck. "Ruth and Mary. They are my sister and mother. They are not Subject A, B, or C, okay?"

"I am sorry, I am just talking the way I would in court."

"As I was saying," he looked over at Martha, "Mary's car not only has the crease, but when magnified, you will see there is a very thin line of rust in the crease and yellow paint. The car in the video has neither the rust nor the paint."

"Is that conclusive?" Furgeson asked.

"This last discovery is conclusive. He rewound the video to the beginning and advanced it frame by frame.

"Then I discovered at one point the mirror on the passenger's side shows an unobstructed view of both the driver and the passenger for just a nanosecond."

An image filled the television screen. There was a reflection in the mirror. It was a woman her mother's age but not her face, and the other woman had purple hair. Her sister did not dye her hair until after the murder.

"This is a fake, a deep fake, an expensive fake, but a fake."

"A fake? Are you sure?" Furgeson asked.

"I will stake my reputation on it."

"Damn!"

"But the gun is in. We can go forward with the case," Furgeson said.

"But the video is out now?" Martha asked.

Furgeson rose and headed for the door. "Yes, I am not taking a fake video into court. I will see you in court."

After the door closed behind him, Farrel said, "That is one piece of evidence shot down. Now we have to look closely at the rest of it."

Chuck turned toward Martha, handed her a business card, and said, "If I can be of any help in the future, call me."

Farrel and Martha were now alone in the office.

Farrel closed the door. "That was a good meeting with a good outcome."

"But he said he was still going forward," Martha said.

"Give him time to think about it. Now that he is looking for it, he might find other problems with the case. So don't give up hope."

"Right. This was just the first shot across the bow."

Martha left the office. She rubbed her head as she returned to her car. The video was no longer a problem. Someone faked it. So why is he going forward with the case? Who paid for an "expensive fake?" Whoever is behind this has money—a lot—but why?

Martha called Ken.

"Ken, it's Martha. I just had a meeting with Spittal."

"I heard, something big is going on. Malroy is off your father's case, and the DA's office is in charge."

"What? When did that happen?"

"Today. They came in and seized all the files. Malroy is on unpaid leave pending an investigation."

"That is big. We need to meet," Martha said.

"I agree. Will you tell Judy? Let's meet at the Bell at 5:00 tonight."

"I will check with her."

Martha returned to the motel and checked out with Scruff. She was moving into her sister's place for now. She also felt it was time to resign from her position in San Antonio—her focus needed to be here.

"Today, Scruff, we are moving. Are you ready? Let me pack up your bowl and food. Wherever your bowl is, is your home, right, old boy?"

She noticed her hands were trembling. Why was she so afraid of her boss? No better time than now. She pulled her cell phone from her pocket and dialed.

"Thank you for calling. Associate Head Librarian Messer speaking.

How may I help you?"

"Hi, Brenda, this is Martha—"

"Martha? I remember a Martha. I think she still works here, but I am not sure. She has not come to work in a long time, and her tasks are piling up."

Why does she always make me feel inferior?

"Brenda, it is I."

"Oh, it is you, the absentee employee. Are you on your way back? You know, to your job."

Brenda, you are making this too easy.

"No, I am not."

"What? You know I cannot hold your job open forever."

"I know. That is the reason for the call. I am resigning my position."

"You—you can't do that! We need you here. I was just joking, please come back."

You have no one to do all your crap jobs you've been shoving off on me.

"I have over two weeks' vacation coming. Take them as my notice."

Brenda huffed into the phone. "What are we supposed to do?"

Martha smiled. "I guess you are going to need to find someone else."

She could always start doing her job and not spending all her time on her phone.

Martha hung up before Brenda could respond.

Good luck, Brenda, finding a librarian who will put up with what I have from you.

She felt lighter as she drove to her sister's apartment. Even Scruff seemed happier as he explored his new digs.

Martha arrived at the Bell thirty minutes before five. She took the booth they had claimed and ordered iced tea. She took a sip of her tea, and her stomach growled.

She glanced at her watch. It had been hours since she last ate. She examined the menu and ordered a steak with a baked potato and a garden salad. To heck with healthy.

She attacked it like Scruff gobbling down his dinner. She wiped a napkin across her mouth, feeling the satisfaction of being comfortably full.

Ken came through the door right at five. He waved and then walked toward her. He looked impressive.

She waved back at him. "So, tell me your news."

Ken placed his order and then turned to Martha. "Late this afternoon, Furgeson came to the station with U.S. Marshals. He was red-faced and looked like he was about to explode. The Marshals took everything on your father's case."

"Then what happened?"

"Then Furgeson spent a few minutes with the chief. They both came out of the office and walked to Malroy's desk."

"Really?"

"Furgeson said, 'No one makes a fool out of me.' The chief took Malroy's gun and shield, and they escorted him out of the building."

"What's up?" Judy said, approaching the booth.

Ken told her everything he had just explained to Martha.

"That will be a surprise for my dad," Judy said.

Martha leaned in and lowered her voice. "Here is what happened today at Farrel's office."

She explained about the deep fake video.

"Wow," Judy said. "This is getting strange."

Ken slid down in his seat. "Did you see who just came in?"

Martha and Judy turned to look.

"Don't look."

"How else are we to see?" Judy asked.

"It's the Phillips—"

"Oh, hi, Mom. Hi, Dad," Judy said.

Elizabeth Phillips waved at her daughter. Then Malroy came from the front of the restaurant and joined the Phillips.

Judy walked over and started talking to her mother. Rick Phillips was in an animated conversation with a friend at a nearby table.

Malroy got up and brushed against Elizabeth's back with his hand as he headed toward the restrooms. She smiled at him.

"Did you see that?" Martha asked.

"Yes. They are no doubt attempting to encourage him after today."

"Not that—the way Malroy touched Elizabeth as he went by her. It was a bit too friendly."

"What are you talking about? Her husband is right there. No."

"You didn't see him touch her?"

"He was just being sociable."

"Okay, but it seemed like more than friendship to me."

Judy returned to the table. "Mom said she had never heard of a deep fake video before—"

Martha's head twisted toward her. "What did you tell her?"

"I'm sorry. I was just talking to her. Did I do something wrong?"

Martha just shook her head slowly. What else had Judy told her mother? Who had her mother told?

The rest of the evening, the conversation was pleasant. Martha watched what she said. Judy was just too quick to talk. She would need to guard what she said, and she would talk to Ken alone from now on.

Martha returned to the apartment and took Scruff for a walk.

Chapter 28

The car's heater was blowing full blast as Ken pulled into the parking lot at the police station. He cringed, climbing out of the warm cocoon of the vehicle and walking through the frigid air to the front door.

"Look at you in a suit," Sally yelled across the parking lot.

"Temporary promotion, filling in for Malroy."

"That is why I am in your car today."

Ken held the glass door open for her. "Take good care of Bertha."

"Bertha?"

"That is what I call my car. She may be old, but she can still get up and go, like my aunt Bertha."

Ken maneuvered through the juggernaut of desks and knocked on the chief's door.

The door opened, and the chief said, "Follow me."

Ken fell in behind her, and together they walked toward Malroy's office. His office looked like a windstorm had blown through, leaving files and loose pages everywhere.

She spread her arms wide. "All his open cases are in here somewhere—everything but the Thomas case. The DA has all that.

See if you can make sense of this."

She walked away, leaving him there staring at the morass of paper.

Sally poked her head in the doorway. "Wow. You need a cup of coffee and a dumpster."

"Thanks."

She was not wrong. A big dumpster.

"Bring you back a coffee?" Sally asked.

"And help me sort through this?"

"Sorry, your promotion, your mess," she said, waving an exaggerated wave.

Ken pushed papers off the stack to make a place for his coffee cup. Where should he start? He guessed just to start with the first stack.

He picked up the first sheet. It was a report of a B and E at the Moon Lite, a dumpy little motel on the east edge of town.

He opened the filing cabinet to file it, only to find a few files in it. That would not help.

Why were these files not digital? That's what he would do. He stacked all the loose papers and took them to the office scanner. He fed them in one by one, and hours later, they were PDF files he could search.

He returned to a desk now cleaned off. He fired up the computer, found his new file, and read the screen.

"What is this?" he said.

He searched through the stack of paper, withdrew one, and went straight to the chief's office.

Ken walked through her door without knocking. "I think you need to see this."

She read it and took off her glasses. "What a shitstorm."

Ken dropped into the chair in front of her desk. "What do we do with it?"

"We have to call the DA, but that will be the last nail in Malroy's coffin."

"He did not tell you about the forensic report?"

She breathed out a sigh. "No, never. You think I would have agreed to go forward with a case if I knew someone planted the fingerprint on the weapon?"

Ken leaned forward in his chair. "Someone faked all the evidence in this case?"

"It is looking like it, and we are looking like the Keystone Cops over here."

"What is your next step?" Ken asked.

"Call the DA and listen to him berate us again."

"Sorry I brought it to you."

"You would have been in more trouble if you had not. While I make my call, you go to a judge and get a release order for the mother and her daughter for lack of evidence."

Ken drove away from the judge's chambers and called Martha.

"I have wonderful news. It looks like your mother and sister will get out of jail today."

"Really? What happened?"

"It looks like all the evidence against them is tainted. If you'd like to meet me at the jail, they will release them in just a few minutes." Ken met Martha in the parking lot outside the county jail.

Martha rushed up to him. "Okay, tell me what happened."

"Wait until we get your family out of here."

They all met in Mary's kitchen.

Martha turned to Ken. "Now, give. Why the sudden change?"

Ruth headed for the bathroom. "I don't care what changed. All I want is a long shower and to sleep in a clean bed."

Mary said, "First, I want a cup of real coffee. The crap they served there looked and tasted like recycled oil. Then I want to hear everything."

She brewed a cup while Martha and Ken waited.

"Now, tell me everything."

Ken lowered his voice. "Malroy failed to disclose the findings of our forensic team and to the DA—"

"What findings?" Martha asked.

"If you give me a minute, I'll get there."

"Okay, don't keep us waiting," Mary said.

"Well, I found a report that said the fingerprint on the gun was planted. It was also faked, and Malroy knew it but did not tell the DA."

"How did Furgeson respond?" Martha asked.

"Your sister and mother are both out," he said.

"Thank God," Mary said.

"So, where do we go from here?" Martha asked.

"What do you mean?" Mary asked.

"About Dad's murder. I know he was not perfect, and he made mistakes, but he deserves more than becoming a cold case collecting dust in a forgotten file room," Martha said.

"I agree, but what can we do? We don't have the computer, the files, or the office," Ken said.

"We could question Malroy. He must know who is doing this," Martha said.

Mary walked toward the door. "Count me out. I have had enough. I am not going back to jail."

"I guess it is just us now," Martha said.

"But do you really think Malroy will tell us anything?" Ken asked.

"All we can do is try."

Ken got up and headed for the door. "I will call on him tomorrow after work. Would you like to come along?"

"You bet."

Ken reached over and kissed her on her cheek. "Don't worry, we will sort this out."

Martha's phone rang at nine o'clock the next morning.

"Martha, this is Ken. You will not believe what happened last night."

She waited for what felt like an eternity. "Well?"

"Malroy is dead," Ken blurted out.

"Deceased? How?"

"I found him this morning at the Moon Lite Motel, the one on the north edge of town."

"What was he doing there?"

"I will talk to you about it at lunch. Can you meet me?"

Martha's hand rubbed the cheek where he had kissed her. "Yes, I will be there. Where?"

Ken said, "The Beef and Bistro. See you there." Martha arrived twenty minutes early.

The server came over. "What will you have?"

"Iced tea with lemon."

"Sweet or unsweetened?"

"Sweet, please."

The server walked away, leaving her alone. What was this news about Malroy? How did he die? Was it suicide? If not, who killed him, and why?

The server returned with the drink. "Are you ready to order?"

"No, I am waiting on someone."

Martha noticed that her hand went back to her cheek.

The server turned on her heels. "Just let me know when they get here."

She hurried off to the table where three young men in suits sat talking. No doubt a business lunch.

Why did Ken kiss me? What did it mean? A kiss on the cheek like a brother and sister, or was there more to it? Am I ready for more?

"Penny for your thoughts."

She turned in her seat to see Ken staring at her.

"You seemed so deep in thought when I came up."

"Just thinking about Malroy," she lied. It was not a complete lie. She had been thinking about him earlier.

"Speaking of Malroy, promise not to breathe a word of this."

Martha looked into his eyes. "I promise."

"We found Malroy dead at the Moon Lite, in his underwear, with three bullets in his chest."

"In his underwear?"

"Yes. The pathologist believes he had sexual relations just before someone shot him—maybe his lover."

"Oh, my God."

"The manager said he checked in at eight last night, by himself."

"By himself?"

"Right. But he has been doing this once a week for months, according to the manager."

"Was it the same night each week?"

"No, that was the weird thing. It would be different nights, different times—sometimes on weekends, others on weekdays."

"You have any idea why? Was he meeting someone?"

"The sex suggests he was, but no idea who. No cameras on the backside of the motel, and he always insisted on a room on the backside. There is an entrance from a back road into the parking lot on that side, of course."

Martha slowly shook her head. "Someone was not happy with Officer Malroy."

"You can say that again, but three bullets? That is overkill."

Martha rubbed the back of her neck. "You have any leads?"

"Nothing, but I will begin by going through his old cases. There might be something in there."

Martha put her head in her hands. "What do we do about Dad? He was the only link we had left."

"I know, but don't give up hope. There has to be something we missed."

Ken looked up. "Do you think there is a link between your father's murder and Malroy's?"

"There might be. It would be worth looking into."

"Our peaceful little town is getting really dangerous. First your father is killed, then Billy, and now Malroy."

Ken glanced at his watch. "I have to get back to work. With Malroy's death, the station is a madhouse. Can we talk again this evening?"

"What time do you get off?"

"Late, I'm afraid. Can I call you?"

Martha nodded. "You have my number. I will wait for your call."

"Would you like a refill on the tea?"

The server was standing there. "He paid the bill on the way out. He is cute. You are a lucky girl."

"Ah, yes. Yes on the tea."

"If I was forty years younger," the server said with a smile.

"Right."

She returned with the tea. "Anything else I can get you?"

"No, I think this will do just fine."

Ken had said maybe they had missed something.

Yes, but what?

Dad had always said, "When faced with a difficult problem, write everything down and the solution might present itself." Thanks, Dad.

She took a napkin and made a list.

Questions that need answers:

1. Who murdered her father?
2. Why was he murdered?
3. Why did someone want to frame Jamal?
4. Who killed Billy?
5. Why?
6. What did he discover?
7. Can we ever find it again?
8. Why frame her mother and sister?

She looked at her list, but it still made little sense. What would her dad do next? He would type out everything into his computer. He had always had a computer. Maybe a computer would help.

She looked at her banking app, checked her balance. She would purchase a computer. Who knows? It might help to see everything on a screen.

She drove to a box store on the edge of town and purchased a mid-price-range laptop. She returned to the restaurant because she had seen a sign that said, "Free Wi-Fi."

She began the setup, and then she connected to her cloud account.

"A cloud account. Of course, Dad would have had a cloud account." She keyed in Ken's number.

"Hi, Martha, I am really busy here. What did you want?"

"I was wondering how to find out if Dad had a cloud account?"

"That is a great idea. Let's talk about it tonight."

She hung up.

She opened the computer and went through the different cloud accounts she knew about. On her third try, she hit pay dirt.

Her father had a OneDrive account.

She opened it and discovered hundreds of files—his sermons, his journals, his illustration files. Scanning through, she came to one called **Office Audio Files.** She clicked on it. A small box appeared in the center of her screen, asking for a password. She used the same password as for his computer that had gotten her into the site. It failed.

She would have to work it out with Ken tonight.

She tried to open his journal file. Same little box, same failure.

So close, yet so far. She closed her new laptop and headed for her car. She pushed the button on the key fob to unlock her doors.

Chapter 29

Martha's phone rang, and Ken suggested they meet at his home to work on the cloud files.

She rang his doorbell a little after seven.

"Let's set up on the kitchen table," Ken said.

Martha placed her laptop on the table.

"What is your password?" She connected to the Wi-Fi.

"What was your dad's password?" Ken asked.

"I don't know. I tried the one for his computer, but it did not work."

"Try reversing it."

Really, can it be that easy?

"I will try it," Martha said. "It worked."

"Did you have any doubt?" Oh, don't be a smart aleck.

She clicked on the file that said **Documents.** Over a thousand icons popped up on the screen.

"How are we ever going to sort through all this?" Martha said.

"We'll have to listen to them one at a time," Ken said. "You want me to order some pizza?"

"At least they are organized by date, so we can start with the newest and work our way back," Martha said. "And the pizza sounds fantastic."

By the time the doorbell rang, they had worked their way through one week of audio files, mostly recordings of conversations between Ruth and Jerry.

"I will grab the paper plates. Would you like a Pepsi?"

Martha shook her head. "That would be great."

She wiped her grease-stained fingers on a napkin and then pushed the button on the computer to play the next file. The room filled with the voice of her father and mother. As she listened, they discussed Christmas. They had planned to travel to see her in Texas as a surprise. Tears started running down her face. They cared. She owed it to her dad to find out what had happened.

"It will take some time to listen to all these files, and it is getting late. Can we take this up again tomorrow?" Ken said.

Martha glanced at her watch. Nine o'clock. "I agree. Let's start fresh tomorrow morning if you are free."

"Day off. Eight o'clock. Is that good for you?"

"Eight it is."

Martha traveled home, made a cup of coffee, and got ready for bed. She slipped on her pajamas, set the computer on the table by her bed, opened the audio application, and listened to more of the files. She lay down and closed her eyes. Listening with her eyes shut, she tried to visualize the action. In her mind, she saw her father sitting in his leather chair, pressing the phone to his ear, scratching notes on a notepad.

She was drifting off to sleep when she heard her father's voice.

"This is Pastor Jerry. We need to talk."

Then there was silence. It must be a phone call. She was only hearing one side of it.

"I know you are busy, but I know what you have been doing."

Another pause.

"I will give you one week to come clean." Another pause.

"This has to stop. Too many people are being hurt." Another pause.

"No, you have one week. No more."

Then silence.

Her eyes sprang open, and she sat bolt upright in bed. This was it. She could feel it in her heart—this was the smoking gun. She grabbed her phone and called Ken.

"Hello," he said sleepily.

"I think I have found it."

"Found what? Do you know what time it is?"

"The file, the reason, the cause—"

"What are you going on about?"

Martha excitedly stood up and started pacing the floor. "I found the reason for Dad's murder."

"What?"

"Can I bring my laptop over and play it for you?"

"Sure. I will get up and make coffee for us."

Martha changed back into street clothes, stuffed the computer into a large bag, and headed for her car.

She pushed the button on her key fob to unlock the doors, placed the bag with the laptop on the backseat, opened the driver's side door, and drove to Ken's apartment.

She opened the back door and reached in to get her laptop. As she bent over, a hand covered her face from behind. A stinging odor filled her nose, and blackness closed in on her. She watched helplessly as her laptop fell to the pavement.

Ken waited for Martha to arrive. He drank one cup of coffee, then a second one. Where was she? She should have been here half an hour ago. He opened the front door and saw her car with the back passenger door standing open.

"What the—"

He walked out and looked inside. Nothing.

A chill ran through his body.

He ran back in, picked up the phone, and dialed 9-1-1. Two minutes later, a police car came screeching to a halt in front of his home.

"What happened here, Ken?" the officer asked as he climbed from his cruiser.

"I don't know, Martha was coming over, but she never showed up."

The officer raised his eyebrows. "She was coming over at 4 o'clock in the morning?"

"She said she had found something I needed to see."

"Well, let's let that go for now. What are we looking at?"

Ken showed him the car and the open door. "Not only is she missing, so is her computer."

"Do you know what was on the computer?"

"She told me she had found the reason for her father's death."

"Okay, take me back to the beginning, Ken."

Ken told him about the files on the computer. "She said she had found the smoking gun."

"You think this abduction was because of the files she found?"

"I am sure of it."

"Do you know who might have her?"

"Harvey Franks. He has been after her since she started looking into her father's murder."

Ken then explained about Franks.

"We need to get our tech people down here, and you need to tell all this to the chief," the officer said.

A Criminal Investigation Site team showed up ten minutes later.

They set up their lights and processed the site.

Ken drove to the station. The chief was waiting for him in her office.

"What is going on?" she asked.

"Martha is missing. I am sure she has been abducted."

"Why?"

"She called me and said she had found a file that explained why her father was murdered."

"What do you suggest we do now, Ken?"

"We need to check any CCTV in the area."

"I agree, and let's hope the CSIs find something at your place."

"Can we get her phone records? Maybe she called someone other than me."

"I will start the process right now."

"You go over and look at our traffic cams and see if you can find her." Ken drove over to the building where they monitored the traffic cameras.

"Hi, Officer Henderson, what are you doing here?" the uniformed woman asked from her seat in front of the screens.

Ken explained about Martha's kidnapping. "I need you to help me find a car."

"Sure. Do you have a time frame?"

"Yes, between 2:30 and 3:00 this morning."

"What make and model are we looking for?"

"I don't know."

"So, what are we looking for?"

"I will have to see if I can discover Martha in one of these cars."

"At least there will not be many cars to look at."

She typed on the keyboard in front of her. "You said to start at 2:30?"

The screens went black for a second, then glowed again with six different intersections.

"Here we go. At 2:36, Martha's car went past the camera. It was followed by a semi-truck. Missed the turn onto the bypass, I'll bet. It happens from time to time," she said.

A black Jeep Pathfinder followed the semi.

"Stop."

"That is not a woman. That man has a beard."

Ken was looking at who he thought was Harvey Franks. He turned the same direction Martha had gone.

"Can we find him on any other cameras?" Ken asked.

"We'll find out."

"Watch that bottom screen. It would be the next one if he does not turn."

They both stared at the screen, but no Martha and no black Jeep.

"That was him, all right."

"Who?"

"Harvey Franks. He is the one who has her."

"Can you get the plate?"

She froze the picture on the screen, typed the keys, and the plate filled the screen.

"Can you give me a copy of the photo?"

"You bet."

She worked the keys again, and a printer came to life on her right side.

"Do you need anything else, Officer Henderson?"

"Ken. Call me Ken. Yes, can you check and see if that Jeep appears again?"

They watched, but no Jeep—not for half an hour.

"Sorry, Ken, I don't see it."

"Neither do I."

"I hope she is okay. I will pray for her."

"Thank you."

"Let me know when you find her."

Ken returned to the station and sent out an APB on the Jeep with the plate number. Then he ran the plate number to find out who it belonged to. He sat at his desk, drumming his finger on the desktop. There had to be something he could be doing. He pulled his keys from his pocket and headed for the chief's office.

"I can't sit here doing nothing. I am going to drive around and see if I can find that Jeep."

"Take a handheld with you in case we hear anything."

"Will do, Chief."

He just began driving up one street and down another, looking in all directions for the black Jeep.

The radio came alive. "Ken here. Did you find her?"

"No, sorry, but the information has come back on the plate. It belongs to a car in Columbus. It is registered to a Honda, not a Jeep. No doubt stolen, but they have officers checking it out right now. I will let you know about any developments."

The radio went dead, and silence filled the car like a smothering blanket.

***

Martha opened her eyes in a dingy room with pealing blue wallpaper with yellow poppies. She tried to wrench her arching arms free from behind her back. She twisted and pulled, but they would not move. After several tries, she gave up. The pain in her upper biceps was unbearable. She had read, if you focus of something else, the pain would decrease. It was worth a try, but what to focus on? How to get out of here?

She tried force her feet apart. No good, they were tied together with ropes. She looked around the room. Nothing was in the room but bed. Plywood covered the single window. The door leading out of the room had the hinges on the other side. They had removed the attached bathroom door. Someone had stripped the bathroom of everything but a toilet.

There was even a hole in the wallboard where a sink had been. The door opened. Framed in the door frame was a tall, breaded man.

"Awake, are we?"

"Yes,"

He walked toward her, "Martha, I have been looking forward to meeting you."

"I am sure you could come up with an easier way, Harvey."

He stopped in mid-stride, "You have been a busy little girl. How did you find my name?"

"Harvey Franks, that is my secret."

He slid a hunting knife from the sheave fastened to his belt, "I don't like secrets, I have spent my life prying secrets out of people."

"Prying?"

He smiled a crooked smile, "Let's say convincing people to share their secrets with me. At least those who lived through our conversations."

Martha's shoulder muscles tightened as she focused on the razor edge of the blade.

"You like my knife, it is great at releasing secrets. Before I leave here, you will beg me to listen to all your secrets."

He waved the knife, like a master chief about to crave a roasted turkey, "My only question right now is," he took steps until he was standing right over her, "Do I get the answers to my questions, or do I rape you first. The boss said, 'I could do anything I wanted to you.'"

She trembled, shaking the bed.

He smiled down at her.

A phone rang. He pulled it from his back jean pocket, "Not now."

He looked at the screen, "Sorry to interrupt our romance, but this is the boss, and the one who pays takes priority."

She listened to the conversation.

"What do you want," he said into the phone.

There was a pause.

"Now!"

Pause.

"Okay, I will be there in fifteen minutes. Don't keep me waiting," he grinned at Martha, "I have exciting plans for this afternoon."

He put the phone and knife away, and started for the door.

Martha looked up from the bed, "Ah, could you release me so I can use the restroom?"

He looked around the room, "No way you can get out of here."

He pulled out the knife and sliced through the ropes around her legs. Then he pulled a key from his jean watch pocket. He put his hands on his right shoulder and ran his fingers down her arm, slowly raking his knuckles over her breast, then down to her hands. He unlocked a pair of handcuffs and dropped them on the bed.

As he stood up, he laughed and said, "Later babe, we will pick up when we left off."

He stood in the doorway, "Be a good girl, or I will be terrible to you."

She heard the door closed, and a lock snapped shut on outside.

She listened as gravel crushed under tires as he drove away.

Martha got up from the bed and looked around. The plywood over the window was screwed to the frame with wood screws. There was a screw every six inches. She tried desperately to get her fingers tips between the wood and the frame. Her fingers ached as she tried to force them between the plywood and the frame. They bled, but it was still not moving.

He had said it would take him fifteen minutes to get where he was going, if it took fifteen minutes to get back, she had thirty, one-half hour to get out of this room. If she was still here when he arrived, he would do what he threatened.

She walked to the restroom. As she feared, there was nothing in there. The water pipes were capped and sticking up through the floor. With bleeding fingers, she tried to twist one of the pipes loose. She grimaced as the pain radiated from her fingertips up her arm.

If she could not leave the room, maybe she could get a weapon. She took hold the pipes and worked at forcing them to twist. She held them tightly and tried again, her hand just continued to slip.

She looked around the room, desperate for anything she could use to tighten around the pipes. There was nothing, nothing at all. No shower curtain, no curtain rod, nothing to fight with. Nothing.

She sat on the bed and cried.

The bed was an old iron bed with pealing paint. It reminded her of the one she slept on at her aunt's house when she and Mary were children. They had been jumping on the bed, and the wooden slates broke and the bed fell to the floor. Wooden slates, maybe this bed also has wooden slates. She lifted the mattress and box springs and saw four wooden slates running across the bed frame.

Could it work, it was her only hope. She pulled one slate from the center of the bed and hide it beside the bed, away from the door. She slid two of the remaining slates to support the head of the bed. Then she positioned the remaining slate at the foot of the bed in a way that the mattress would fall through to the floor with enough weight on it.

She heard the gravel from outside. She positions herself on the bed and waited.

The door to the bedroom opened and Harvey Franks came in and walked toward her.

Chapter 30

Ken rushed through the door of the Chief's office. The Chief stood up from her desk and walked over to him.

"Have you heard anything yet?" Ken asked.

"No, we've heard nothing at all. Every unit is out looking and following up on every lead. We won't leave a single stone unturned. We will find her."

She sounded positive, but the lines on her face told another story.

"Is there anything else I need to know about?" Ken asked.

"Yes, Rachelle from ballistics called and said she needs to see you immediately."

Ken hurried to his car and drove three blocks to the new ballistics laboratory on the edge of town. He burst through the door. A worker who had been there for years met him.

"What's up, Ken?"

"I got a call that Rachelle wants to see me. Do you know what's going on?"

"No, but she's down the hall in her office. Go on down."

Ken walked through the hall of the new building and came to the hollow-core door with a sign that read **Ballistics.**

Rachelle was sitting at her desk, her glasses pushed up on her head as she read a file. Ken guessed Rachelle to be in her forties, with black hair and fine silver highlights earned with age.

"Rachelle, it's Ken Henderson. Do you have a minute for me?"

She laid down the papers, smiled, and reached across to her inbox, picking up a red folder. She opened it and handed it to him.

He read. "Are you sure?"

"I ran the test twice. The same type of gun was used in the homicide of Reverend Thomas, Billy, and now Detective Malroy. The shooter used a different barrel, but the cartridges all had the same firing pin marks. Also, the same pattern—three rounds in the chest."

"Same shooter. So, they're connected."

"That's what it looks like," she said.

"You know this changes everything. We're now looking for a serial killer. How do you think they're connected?"

"That's your job. I'm not a detective—I'm a ballistics expert. I've done my job. Now you need to do yours."

She paused, "Have you heard anything about Martha?"

Ken rubbed his hand across his brow. "No, but the Chief says everybody is out looking for her, and I'm going to get back on the road myself. The only description we have is that she's in a black jeep."

Rachelle smiled. "Well, keep me informed. You have my number. Please call me if there's anything I can do to help." Ken drove back toward the police station.

"We need to look for something that connects them."

"Since Jerry's death was first, clearly he is the line that we need to investigate fully."

She turned towards her office, saying over her shoulder, "If I can be of any help, call me."

Ken went into the break room, dropped a couple of quarters into the coffee machine, and purchased a large black coffee. Sally came around the corner, and he asked, "Would you also like a cup?"

"Yes, if you don't mind," she said, sitting down at a table. "Have you heard anything about Martha yet?"

"No, but the Chief has assured me everything is being done."

"I'm sure the Chief is doing everything she can do. I know that all the units are looking for that Jeep. It's only a matter of time, right?"

"Yes, but time we don't have."

The Chief came busting through the door into the cafeteria. "Ken, I'm glad I caught you. The State Patrol just called and said they have located Martha's phone. She just turned it on."

Ken, the Chief, and Sally all went into her office. She picked up the phone that was sitting on her desk and punched the button for the speakerphone. A voice came on the speaker.

"This is Patrolman Michael. As I was telling your Chief, we have located Martha's phone. It was just activated a few minutes ago. We triangulated its signal. She was at the McDonald's just off Highway 35, and now she is driving down US 35 North."

They all went to their vehicles and headed for US 35 North. They came up behind a black Jeep traveling 55 miles an hour. Ken turned on his lights, and the Jeep slowly edged to the side of the road. Ken and the Chief both got out of their cars and walked toward the black Jeep.

Ken drew his Glock and aimed at the tinted window on the driver's side. "Driver, roll down your window and place both your hands outside where I can see them!"

The window on the Jeep slowly went down, and two hands came through the opening. Two ancient, very wrinkled, and shaky hands emerged. Ken was looking down his sights to find he was pointing his pistol at one of the senior citizens from Brownsville.

He holstered his weapon. "Miss, please step out of the vehicle."

"Yes, Officer. What did I do? I just went to McDonald's for a Big Mac. It's my only real vice. I know the doctor doesn't want me to do it, but I never dreamed he'd call the police."

The Chief put her arms around the distraught woman and led her back to her car, putting the shaken woman in the back seat. About that time, the State Patrol arrived as backup, and one of the officers said, "I thought we were picking up a serial killer, and instead, we apprehended Granny Smith."

"But Martha's phone has to be here somewhere," Ken said. He took his phone from his pocket and dialed her number. They heard a faint ringing.

"It is coming from the rear of the Jeep," Ken said.

He walked toward the back of the vehicle. The ringing got louder and louder. He climbed underneath and found the phone wedged between the gas tank and the body of the car.

"It was just a distraction!"

Chapter 31

Martha heard the crunch of gravel in the driveway outside the house. She tried to lay perfectly still while waiting for Harvey to come back. She did not want the bed to fall early. She didn't have to wait long. She heard the lock on the outside of the bedroom door being removed, and then his bulky figure filled the doorframe. His eyes scanned her body from head to toe. He walked toward her with a crooked smile.

Martha shook uncontrollably. *Oh God, don't let the bed fall yet, not until he is on it.*

"Are you trembling because you are afraid or because you are excited? Either is good for me."

He came to the edge of the bed, sat down, and reached across her trembling body. He unbuttoned the first button of her blouse as she waited for the bed to drop.

"I see you decided I won't need this," he said, putting his hand on the handle of the knife on his belt. He unbuttoned the second button on her blouse.

Fall, bed. Why hasn't it fallen? His entire weight was already on it.

She rocked her head violently and screamed, "No, no, no!"

He just laughed at her distress, and in spite of her struggling, he unbuttoned the third button on her blouse.

Just then, the bed collapsed. He fell toward the foot of the bed. She reached over, snatched the 1x3 wooden slat that she had hidden beside the bed, and brought it down as hard as she could on top of his head. A horrible thud filled the room. He raised up like a wounded bear. His face turned bright red. His eyes bulged. Then he dropped on top of her.

She wiggled to free herself from his heavy weight. She stood and saw that he had a major gash on the crown of his head. She used the handcuffs that had been used on her to put his arms behind his back. She tied his feet together, winding the rope several times around his ankles and tying it tight. She rooted around in his pockets until she found the key fob for the vehicle outside. She glanced back one last time. He was bleeding profusely from his head. I can't leave him like that.

She went into the kitchen and looked for any towels she could use. She found a few small dishtowels but nothing big enough for what she needed. Searching through the rest of the house, she found a bathroom where there were bath towels in the closet. She took one of the larger towels back to her former prison and wrapped it tightly around his head. She tied it in such a way that it would at least slow the bleeding.

As she left the bedroom, she glanced back and said, "I'll send some help back for you."

Afraid that time was running out, she made her way outside. Seeing the black Jeep, she pushed the button on the key fob and heard the doors unlock. She got inside, turned the key, and the vehicle roared to life. She put it in gear and drove out. As she reached the end of the driveway, she hesitated.

Do I go left or right?

She waited for just a second, knowing that time was of the essence.

I'll go right. She turned right, not knowing for sure where she was going or if she would run across the boss. If he was on his way, if he had already come that way—she definitely did not want to see him. As she drove, she noticed a button for the voice recognition system on the steering wheel.

She pushed it, and a sweet feminine voice came through the speakers. "How can I help you?"

She said, "Directions to Brownsville Police Department."

The voice responded, "It's twenty-five minutes to your destination." Suddenly, the screen in the middle of the dashboard filled with a map.

She followed the directions, heading toward the police department. She pulled in twenty-five minutes later. Ken saw her across the office and came running. He grasped her, pulled her close into his arms, and held her so tightly she felt the warmth of his body. For the first time in a long time, she felt safe.

She reveled in his strength.

She explained to the chief where she had left Harvey Frank and how she had left him.

"I put him in cuffs. He's got rope tied around his ankles, and he has a major head wound. You need to get there with an ambulance as soon as possible."

Ken stayed with her while the Chief and Sally went to the house Martha had directed them to. Thirty minutes later, the Chief returned to the office and walked over to Martha.

"Tell me again how you left him," the Chief said.

"Like I said, he was handcuffed, tied up, and he had a wound on his head."

"We found him just like you said. Almost." Martha's stomach dropped.

"Almost?"

"He was on a broken-down bed, he was handcuffed, and his feet were tied. He had a major wound on his head, like you said. But there were three bullet holes in his chest."

"I didn't kill him."

"So, he was alive when you left?"

"He was alive. He was breathing. He was wounded, but he was alive."

"Martha, we're going to protect you until we figure out what's going on. Somebody wants you out of the picture."

Ken agreed to take Martha home. As they were driving, he said, "The Chief told me to stay with you no matter what."

"I hope that won't interfere with everything else you're doing."

Martha knew her voice was trembling, but she couldn't control it. She could not believe how frightened she felt. As they drove along, a car beside them honked its horn, and Martha jumped.

"Are you okay?" Ken asked.

"I'm fine. It's just... I just can't… I'm fine."

They arrived at the house and found Mary and Ruth waiting for them.

"How are you, darling?" Ruth said as they walked through the door.

"Ouch!" Ken said.

Martha looked down and saw she was squeezing his arm too tightly.

"I'm sorry, I didn't mean to hurt you."

As Martha sat down on the couch, she felt her body trembling. Ken sat beside her and wrapped his sinewy arms around her shoulders.

"Would anyone enjoy a cup of coffee?" Mary asked.

"Coffee would be lovely," Martha said.

"I hope we are done with this foolishness. Now, I hope you've learned to stay away from whatever this problem is. You cannot do this anymore. You girls are too important to me," Ruth said.

Martha sat there, feeling the warmth of Ken's body transferring to hers. Even though she was afraid, there was a sense of safety and security she hadn't felt in over a year. It was a feeling she didn't think she would ever find again. She wasn't sure if she wanted to find it again.

Mary came in with two cups of coffee, one for Ken and one for Martha.

"I think I'm going to bed," said Ruth as she waddled off toward the back of the house.

Martha looked at Ken, and even through her fear, she said, "Who do you think the boss is?"

"We don't have to think about that right now," Ken said.

Martha knew that until she figured out who the boss was, who had killed her father, and who had abducted her, she could not relax. She would never sleep a full night until whoever it was brought to justice.

"Do you think it would help if we looked at possibilities?" Martha asked.

Ken said, "What we do at the station is build a crime board. I could run down to the mall and pick up a large whiteboard, and we could see what's going on."

Martha nodded. "That would be a great idea."

Ken smiled. "Do you think you'll be okay until I get back?" "Certainly. I have Mom here and my sister. Nobody's going to bother me here."

Ken left for the mall, and Mary sat down beside Martha, pulling her into a tight hug.

"I was so worried for you," Mary whispered. "I can't tell you how scared I was."

"I was scared; I wasn't sure I was going to survive. It was so bad, Mary."

"What happened?"

"He took me into the bedroom, he handcuffed me, and then… And then he, he planned to rape me."

"I cannot believe how bad it was for you."

"Mary, I've never been so scared in all my life. He said we were going to have fun."

"So, you say someone shot him?"

"Mary, I would have if I'd had a gun. But I didn't have the gun, thank God."

They sat there in silence, drinking their coffee.

Ken returned with the whiteboard and set it on the couch. He also had purchase markers, and he wrote the name, "Pastor Jerry." A few inches over he wrote, "Detective Malroy, and Billy." Then he drew a line between them. On the left-hand side of the board he wrote, "Fake video and, "fake fingerprint on the gun." On the right-hand side of the board he wrote, "Mary carried off," and "Martha's abduction." Underneath that he wrote in big, bold capital letters, "WHO," with a question mark.

He said "Let us write everything we know. Let's start with the fake video. What do we know about the fake video?"

"It had to cost a lot of money according to the expert," Mary said.

"And they had to have access to pictures of mom and Mary and Mary's car." Martha said.

"What else do we know about the fake video?" Ken asked.

There was a long pause and then Mary said, "And they had to know about Sarah Richards. They had to know about the connection."

"That's right," Ken said.

"And what about the fake fingerprint?"

"Well, they had to understand about forensics," Ken said.

"And they knew what kind of gun was used in the murder?" Mary asked.

"Can either of you think of anything that would connect your father to Billy and Malroy?" Ken asked.

"Billy, yes, but not Malroy," Martha said.

"There is nothing, nothing that I know," Mary said. "There's one more thing that needs to be on the board."

"What is it?" Ken said.

"Dad's files, the audio files."

"Of course, especially the one you were going to show me." Ken said.

"If you're up to it. Let's listen to those files again and see if we can figure out who is behind this," Ken said.

Ken drove back over to his apartment and picked up his computer and returned to the house. Mary made coffee for everyone while Ken connected the computer to a hot-spot using his phone. They listened to the files one by one. First, Mary played for them both the file that she had found before her abduction.

"I see what you mean by it is a smoking gun," Ken said.

"But only if we can figure out who is on the other end of that phone call," Martha said.

Mary said, "Maybe if we listen to the rest of them. We will figure it out."

"Well, I'm game," Ken said.

After they had listened to about thirty more files, they came to a Pre-marriage counseling file. The Pre-marriage counsel was Judy. Martha recognized her voice immediately.

In the middle of the conversation Judy said, "My dad has been sleeping with me since I was twelve years old."

"Oh, my God," Martha said, "Did you hear that!"

"Now that is a real smoking gun," Ken said.

Mary shook her head and said, "I can hardly believe what I heard."

"No wonder dad had said he would only give one week to resolve this," Martha said, "Rick has to be the person of the other end of that phone call."

"The recording is powerful, but to be honest, it's not enough," Ken said.

"What else do we need?" Martha asked.

"We are going to need a confession or we are going to need Judy to confirm it." Ken said.

"We need to see Judy," Martha said.

"But that will wait until tomorrow. You need a good night's sleep now. I will bed down on the couch right here," Ken said.

Chapter 32

Martha woke early the next morning. She patted her way into the kitchen and got a cup of coffee. Ken was already there, drinking a cup of coffee.

"Are you going to call Judy today so that we can visit with her?" Ken asked.

"I do plan to call Judy in just a few minutes; however, I think it might be better if I went to visit her alone."

"But the chief said I am to stay with you no matter what."

"I'm not sure she will open up before both of us. You know this is a really sensitive subject and very embarrassing for her. I think it would be best if I went to see her alone."

"Why don't you set up a place to meet and I'll just stay in the car."

"I'm going to call her in just a few minutes and maybe we can meet either at the restaurant, or possibly at the library."

"I don't care where you meet as long as I can see you from the car."

Martha retrieved her phone from her pants pocket and looked up Judy in her contact list.

"Hi, Judy, how are you doing today?"

"Just fine, why did you call?"

Martha was afraid to move directly into the reason for her call, but she didn't want to waste time. "Would it be possible for us to get together later this morning?"

There was a pause on the phone and then Judy said, "Yes, can it wait until after the breakfast rush? We could meet here at the restaurant, say 10:30?"

"10:30 would be great."

Martha showered, dressed, and asked Ken to drive her over to the restaurant. She left the car, went into the restaurant, and sat at a booth where Ken could see her from the parking lot.

Judy came over and sat down, "What is it you wanted to talk about?"

Martha said, "We need to talk about what you told my father."

There was a long silence followed by Judy saying, "Your father, what are you talking about?"

"Judy, are you going to make me spell it out?"

"I'm not sure what you're referring to."

"I'm talking about what you said to my dad during your premarital counseling session about what your father was doing to you."

Judy's face reddened, a torrent of tears came to her eyes, and started tracing their way down her cheek.

Martha reached her hand over and rested it her on Judy's hand, "I know it's hard," she said, "But it's really important that you tell me everything."

"But it is so embarrassing," Judy said through her tears.

"I just need you to be honest with me about what has been happening at your house?"

Judy wept heavily and Martha slid around in the booth and wrapping her arms around her shoulders, pulling Judy close to her, and letting her cry.

After she had wept for a few minutes Judy said, "I told your father because, because he was eating me up on the inside. I couldn't live with it anymore. And he didn't judge me. He just told me he would try to help."

"Who have you told about what's going on besides my father?" Martha said.

"No one, honest, I haven't told a soul besides your father."

"So would you be willing to go to the police and tell them what's been going on."

Judy rocked her head, "No, never, it would be too dangerous. Martha, you don't understand my dad is a very powerful man."

"Even if I go with you and promise you protection?"

"He may be wrong and what he's doing maybe, well sick, but he is my dad."

"But it's hurting you and your family."

"But I'll do nothing to hurt my family, there's nothing more important than family. Martha, understand that. I will never betray my family."

Judy took the towel that was hanging on her apron, wiped her tears, stood up. Judy jabbed her finger into Martha's face and said through clenched teeth, "This conversation is over."

Stomping off towards the kitchen, she left Martha sitting there alone. She knew for sure it was true.

She returned to the car and Ken asked, "What did you find out?"

"I learned that the abuse is true. But I also learned that Judy is never ever going to testify. She is scared to death of her father."

Ken drove her back to Mary's home.

Martha laid in bed that night with Scruff, "If Judy won't testify then I guess I am going to have to convince Rick to admit the abuse. But how can I possibly get him to admit what he's been doing all these years? What do you suggest old fellow?"

Scruff cuddled in beside her and fell asleep.

***

The next morning, Martha and Ken called Rick Phillips' office.

"Good morning, how may I help you?" came the singsong voice of the receptionist over the phone.

"My name is Martha Thomas and I would like- "

"Martha, I was told to expect your call. The Senator told me to clear his next available opening. Are you available for 3 o'clock this afternoon?"

"He told you to expect my call?"

"Yes, and will that nice police officer, Mr. Henderson be accompanied you as well?"

"Yes," Martha said slowly.

"We will look forward to seeing today at 3 o'clock with Mr. Henderson."

The phone went dead and Martha's just sat and stared at her screen.

Ken came up behind her and ask, "Is Rick willing to see you? I expect he's probably going to block you at every point."

"On the contrary, he told the secretary to expect my call and she ask if you would come with me."

"That is not what I expected at all," Ken said

Martha and Ken were driving towards Columbus. She needed to merge onto the highway. She sped up and pulled her car in between two semi-trucks.

"What do you expect him to say when you get there?" Ken asked.

"I confess I'm really not sure. I was a little taken back when the secretary said she had been expecting my call, and that she knew you would come with me. Also, it makes little sense to me. I'm confused still."

"I don't expect them to admit anything."

Martha hustled to pass the semi, "Have you learned anything in the investigation my father's death yet."

"Just another puzzle piece that doesn't seem to fit. We knew that Billy, and Malroy had both been shot with the same gun and now we find out that Harvey was shot with the same gun."

"You mean the man that kidnapped me?"

"We just got the ballistics back today before we left. They said that it was definitely the same weapon."

Martha was silent as she continued to drive. Same weapon, same killer. What would link them together? What link could an author, a police detective, and a spook have in common? If we can understand that question, we have a good chance of figuring this whole thing out.

They arrived at Rick's office and rode the elevator up to his suite. As they open the door, the secretary looked up from her desk and smiled sweetly, "You must be Martha and this young man with you must be officer Henderson."

Martha moved right up to the front of her desk, "We're here to see Rick."

She pulled a plastic tray from a drawer in her desk and pushed it towards them "Yes, he's waiting for you. If you don't mind, he asked me to make sure that you don't bring any phones or recording devices in. So, if you will just put your phones and any other recording devices in this tray, I'll be glad to give them to you when you leave. It's a precaution we often take."

Martha looked at Ken. Ken raised his eyebrows, however, he reached into his pocket and pulled out his phone and placed it in the plastic tray. Martha also took her phone and dropped it inside the tray.

"We understand, Mr. Henderson or do you prefer officer Henderson."

"Mr. is fine."

"We understand, Mr. Henderson, that you will want to keep your firearm, but we need you to sign a statement saying that you will not repeat anything that is said at this meeting, along with you Miss."

"Again, this is a normal precaution, especially when dealing with a setting senator. And you know he's running for president, right?"

Martha grinned, "Yes, I believe we've heard that."

The secretary punched a button on her phone, and said, "Senator, your visitors are here."

A few seconds later, the door to his office opened and a young man in his thirty's dressed in khaki pants, light blue pullover sweater and his hair perfectly combed, step through the door, "I am the Senator's campaign manager. If you will follow me, they're waiting for you inside."

They are waiting for us inside. Who else is at this meeting?

Martha stomach did flip-flops as she walks through the door and saw inside the room, Rick, his wife Elizabeth, an older man with graying black hair, dressed in a pinstripe suit, that probably cost more than her last car, and the young man that had led them into the office.

"We don't want you to feel ganged up on, but we felt we all have an interest in this meeting," Rick said as he stood behind his desk and extended his right hand.

Martha ignored the hand and sat down in the overstuffed leather seat in front of the desk. Ken, however, shook his hand and took his seat.

"No reason we can't be civil, "Rick said as he took his seat.

Elizabeth rose from her seat and stood behind the desk with her hands resting on the glass surface of the desk staring over into Martha's eyes.

"I am sure this meeting has something to do with what Judy mistakenly said to your dear father."

We are going to get right into it. No beating around the bush, no asking if we want coffee.

Martha leaned forward in her seat and said, "Yes, we would like to discuss what Judy said."

The older man with salt-and-pepper hair stood up and said, "I want you to completely understand this meeting is off the record. And we will deny anything what is said here, if repeated. We will sue you, and your family, if you whisper a word of what said in this meeting ever."

Rick put his hand up and motioned for the older man to sit down, "That's lawyer speak for we will not admit anything after this meeting."

Elizabeth was clearly disturbed as she pounded her fist on the table and rolled her eyes, "Let's get on with this. I have a meeting to chair with the Heart Association and I will not be late."

Rick said, "My wife is deeply committed to taking care of the charities that she's volunteered for."

Martha looked at Elizabeth and said, "So what about what Judy said to my father, is it true?"

Elizabeth looked at her and smiled and said, "Dear do you know the number one reason politicians fail?"

"I don't know, scandals?"

"Not just any scandals, but sexual scandals. That's what almost brought down the Clinton's, and you see a politician falling every day because they simply can't keep it in their pants. Rick here had that problem early in his career, I caught him in bed with a 13-year-old girl."

Rick squirmed uncomfortably as a flush spread across his face. Martha looked at the other people in the room and they were completely stone-faced.

"She was one of Judy's friends. After I took care of that problem, I decided Rick would never need to look outside his home for his, shall we say, his sexual needs. That very night, I told him he did not need to look outside his own home, his own family was there to satisfy him."

"But that is incest, and it's perverted." Martha blurted out.

"Grow up, girl. Soon it's going to be legal. It won't be long before they're going to push for legal sex with minors, and the legalization of what you call incest will follow."

Ken stood up and said, "It's illegal now and it will be illegal forever."

Elizabeth slowly shook her head no, "The laws will change. People we see us as ahead of the curve, when my husband becomes president, no one will remember, or care."

Martha couldn't believe her ears, she not only knew about it and approved of it, but she also promoted it.

Martha asked, "But what about what it's doing to your daughter Judy?"

"She is learning sex is a tool that we women need to exploit to get ahead. I'm proud to say Rick here has never had a sexual scandal in his entire career. When he wants a woman, he comes home and one of us takes care of him."

"This is disgusting," Martha said.

Martha looked around at everyone in the room, the lawyer was just staring straight ahead as if he had heard nothing. The young man also seemed totally uninterested in the conversation. Elizabeth and Rick were both grinning.

"The very best thing you can do, young lady," the lawyer said, "Is to forget this entire conversation. I assure you if you mention anything that was said here today, we will destroy you. A setting senator is a powerful person. Officer Henderson you will never get a job as a police officer ever again. Martha, you will never work in a public library again. I believe we understand each other. Now this meeting is over."

"But what about what happened to my dad?" Martha said.

"Don't expect us to admit to a first-degree murder," Elizabeth said, "In this meeting or any other. Now I have to be off to my charity meeting, you two have a good drive back home."

***

Martha and Ken drove in stunned silence.

"You know he can do it?" Ken said after ten minutes.

"Do what?"

"Destroy us, at least our careers."

"What about the injustice, what about Judy?"

"If she will not tell the authorities, there's not much we can do."

"What about my father?"

"We don't know for sure that this has anything to do with your father. There's no actual link that we found to your father's death, to any of the deaths."

"Do you think I should have another go at Judy?"

"You could try, but I think it's going to turn out the same way, Rick is a powerful man, and no one is going to oppose him, including his daughter."

He's probably right, no one would go against Rick. He is already the most powerful man in the entire state of Ohio, and if elected as President, he will be the most powerful man in the world. The only hope would be a member of the family to have the courage to speak the truth. And right now, that is in short supply.

She pulled into the parking lot. They went into the house. Mary met them at the door, "Well?"

Ken said, "We really can't talk about what happened at the meeting," as he looked over at Martha.

Martha shook her head yes and said, "Let's just say it didn't go as we expected."

So, what do I do now, what is my next step? I can't let this rest, but there is not anything that I can point to that will change what's already happened.

"I hope your adventure into being a detective is over now," Ruth said as she came into the kitchen.

The next morning, Ken went back over to his apartment and grabbed some clothes so he would have something to change into.

Martha was drinking a cup of coffee when her phone ring, "Martha Thomas here."

"Martha, this is Jacqueline, could we meet? I'm terrified."

"What is wrong?"

"My dad and mom are going to be coming home from Washington DC today and they are furious."

"Where would you like to meet?"

"How about at the Dinner Bell?"

"I can meet you about 10 o'clock."

"Can you come alone, this is really embarrassing, and I don't want anybody else to hear what I have to say."

Martha glanced down at her watch, "Yes I'll meet you at the dinner bell 10 o'clock alone."

Martha wondered what she would want. Maybe she was going to be the family member that finally broke the secret open. At least they were meeting at a public place, not much could happen inside a public restaurant.

Martha drove over to the Dinner Bell at 9:45 and waited in her car until Jacqueline pulled up beside her.

Jacqueline pulled her car in beside Martha's, walked over to the driver's window, and then rapped on the window. Martha lowered the window, "Can we talk out here in your car?"

Martha fired up the engine of the car and she reached over and flipped the switch to unlock the doors. Jacqueline slid into the passenger seat.

"It is freezing out there," Jacqueline said.

"The weather reporter just said it's ten above zero, but it feels like it's two below," Martha said as she reached for the heater control and turned it to full blast.

"Would you like a cup of coffee?" Jacqueline asked, "I'll be happy to go in and get us one."

While Jacqueline was inside the restaurant getting two cups of coffee, Martha continued to heat the inside of the car. When Jacqueline returned and opened the door, a polar blast of air entered the cabin, she quickly shut it and said, "Thank you for coming out to talk to me. I was so worried. I just didn't know who else I could call."

"You can always talk to me," Martha said.

"It's been so hard, you know what my father's been doing is not right but, but I still loving."

"Just because you love him doesn't mean you have to put up with what's going on," Martha said.

For the next twenty-five minutes, tears rained down Jacqueline's cheeks as she opened up and explain all the abuse that she had endured since she was twelve years old.

"I've written it all down," Jacqueline said, "It's in all my diaries that are all back at the house."

Martha said, "do you think it's about time we go to the police."

Jacqueline, through her sobs, said, "Yes, can we swing by my house and pick up the diaries?"

Martha said, "Sure."

Jacqueline said, "Can you follow me over to my house and I'll leave my car at the house, and I can go with you to the police station."

Martha drove to the Phillips' house following Jacqueline when they arrived, they went inside Jacqueline says said, "My diaries are up in my room."

"What time are your parents getting home?"

"We still have two hours."

She climbed the stairs. Martha fell in behind her climbing the curved staircase until they reached the second floor and then they walked down the carpeted hallway to the room with a sign on it that was hand carved that said Jacqueline.

Jacqueline motioned for Martha to take a seat on the bed saying, "If you wait right here, I'll dig out my diaries, they are in my closet."

She handed a leather-bound journal to Martha and said, "Would you read this and see if it sounds too to foolish?"

Martha read. The grammar and the spelling were second rate, but the emotions in the words were overwhelming. She sensed a strange combination of pain and pride in the writing.

Martha noticed that one page was turned down, she flipped there out of curiosity and started to read.

"Today is the day that I've been waiting for, today is the day that I fix the screwup of my sister Judy. I drove over to Pastor Thomas' house, rang the doorbell to his office. When he opened the door, I shot him three times. I really didn't want to hurt the old man, but as mother always says, 'There's nothing more important than family.'"

Martha looked up from the journal to see Jacqueline standing in the doorway, one hand on her hip, and the other holding a Sig Sauer, 9 mm pistol aimed at her chest.

***

Ken arrived back at Mary's apartment with two freshly pressed uniforms hanging from his hooked finger as he walked up the sidewalk. He noticed that Mary's car was gone.

He opened the door and asked, "Where's Mary."

Mary came walking in from the kitchen holding the cup of coffee, "Right here."

"I noticed your car was gone. I thought perhaps you'd gone to work."

"No, Martha borrowed it. She had to go down to the Dinner Bell to meet someone."

"Why did she take off without asking me? She knows that I have to answer the chief about her whereabouts. I wish, just for once, she would do what she's been told to do."

Ken's phone rang, he hoped it was her calling. He pulled his phone from his jean pocket and spoke.

"This is the chief. The son of the manager at the motel says he knows who it was that was visiting with Malroy. I want you to drive over and find out what he is talking about."

Ken drove to the motel, walked inside, and waited for the manager to come out.

"My chief says that you know who was visiting Malroy," asked Ken.

"Not me, was my boy. I had him out there cleaning the parking lot and he said he saw the girl that came in."

The manager called his son from the back room who walked out, looked up at Ken and said, "Hi, you must be the police officer."

Ken said, "Can you describe the person who you saw going into Malroy's room."

"Like I told my Pop, I have seen her before, right here in the newspaper."

The kid handed Ken a copy of the Brownsville papers, "She's right there." He pointed his chubby little finger at a picture of the Phillips' family.

Ken pointed at Elizabeth, "You mean her?"

"Not her. Her," he said pointing at the picture of Jacqueline, "She was the one I saw going into the room."

"Thank you, you were a great help."

Ken returned to his car, radioed the Chief, "The child identified Jacqueline Phillips."

"Jacqueline, she's only a child, she can't be much over nineteen years old."

"That's what I thought, but he was certain it was her that went into the motel room with Malroy the day he was shot."

"Why don't you and Martha come on down here to the station and we will figure out how we handle this additional information."

"Chief, Martha went over to the dinner bell to visit someone, I'm going to drive over there and pick her up."

"You make sure you find her immediately. We don't know what Jacqueline will do."

Ken drove with the sirens blaring over to the Dinner Bell where he found no Martha nor Jacqueline.

He went in and asked the manager, "Have you seen Martha or Jacqueline today?"

"Jacqueline came in to grab a couple cups of coffee to go. I would've sworn Martha was setting out in her car waiting. Next thing I knew, they were both gone."

"Do you have any idea where they may have gone?"

"No, it got really busy here. When I looked out again, both cars were going."

Ken returned to his car, he keyed his radio, and said, "Put out an APB for Jacqueline Phillips."

Ken returned to the police station and walked into the chief's office. The chief was busy on the phone, waved him into a seat. After she hung up, she asked, "Did you find Martha?"

"No Chief, but I believe she is with Jacqueline."

"Why?"

"The manager at the restaurant said he saw them together this morning and both their cars disappeared about the same time."

"I think it's time we call the state police and see if they can triangulate her phone, "the Chief said.

"I'm already on it," Ken said as he walked out the door.

The state patrol called and said, "We have triangulated the phone's location, it is currently at 1217 Snow Hill Dr."

"That is the Phillips' place," Ken said.

The Chief said, "You head over there, I'm sending back up!"

Chapter 33

Martha's entire body tensed, and her mouth dropped open as she stared down the barrel of the 9 mm, "What is this all about?"

Jacqueline grinned and waved her gun towards Martha's coat, "You better grab your jacket. It is going to be cold outside."

Martha draped her jacket over her arm and led the way through the hallway and down the hand carved staircase to the front door with Jacqueline close behind, the 9 mm not wavering.

"Last chance, put your jacket on," Jacqueline said, struggling to put her own jacket on without losing the grip on the 9 mm.

Martha reluctantly slid her arms into the winter coat and opened the front door. They made their way across the porch, down the stairs, and behind the house. They had walked about a hundred yards when they came to a wooded area.

"Through there!" Jacqueline demanded.

"You don't have to do this."

"You don't understand, I have to. I like you Martha, but I have to protect the family, there is nothing more important than family."

"You're the one that shot my father."

"Yes, with this gun. With part of this gun, this model has an exchangeable barrel. That barrel was in the pistol Malroy hid in the ashes of your home. He would do anything for me. I didn't want to shoot your dad, but he could have ruined my family. I will do anything to protect my family. Did you know I'm going to be the daughter of the President of the United States? I would not let an old, retired preacher, or a police detective, or even you stand in the way. I can see it now. Daddy president, mama first lady, and me and Judy, standing there on the balcony at the White House."

They moved through the woods and Jacqueline stepped on a frozen branch that gave way with her weight, and she fell, losing the gun. Martha ran as hard as she could to get deep into the woods. A loud explosion echoed through the trees and a tree beside her exploded in a shower of bark and splinters. Martha dodged to her left and kept moving.

"I will find you!" Jacqueline screamed.

Martha hid behind a giant oak tree as Jacqueline searched. She was less than twenty feet away when Martha heard the sirens coming.

"It's over, Jacqueline! Can't you hear the police."

"They are always running around out here. No one knows you're here, Martha."

Martha reached into her pocket as she whispered, "Oh, God. Help me!"

She felt the cross pin in her pocket that her father had kept in his desk. This is my only weapon, it's not much, but it might work. She twisted the cross pin so that the point came out and she wrapped it in her gloves. She picked up a rock. Threw it over top of Jacqueline's head. It landed a few feet on the opposite side. Jacqueline turned and fired in the sound's direction. At that same moment, Martha ran as hard as she could and stabbed Jacqueline in the back with the pen, pushing it in as deep as she could. The blood flowed.

Jacqueline bellowed. The gun went off again.

Jacqueline, now with the pen sticking out of her back three inches, bleeding profusely, struggled with Martha for the gun. The gun was between them. Martha had her fingers on it. Jacqueline and Martha were rolling around, each pulling and pushing, striking out at each other. Suddenly the gun went off. Martha felt a burning, terrible pain in her chest. Everything went black. She could feel herself losing consciousness. Then nothing.

Ken arrived at the house and started pounding on the door. He heard a gunshot come from behind the house. Pulling his Glock from its holster, he barreled towards the sound.

He looked around desperately for any sign of them. He glanced around the yard. Another gunshot sounded.

Fear gripped him, his stomach was in knots, and his heart raced. He screamed, "Martha, Martha!"

He ran flat out into the woods towards the sound. He heard yet another crack of the gun. His stomach sank. Three shots, just like Rev. Thomas.

He came upon the scene and cried. Martha lay there, underneath the weight of Jacqueline. It was a grotesque scene. The pin sticking out of Jacqueline's back, blood flowing all over both of them, neither of them were moving. Was he too late, were they both dead? He slowly and carefully, with his gun pointing at Jacqueline, lifted her off Martha. Jacqueline wept as a crimson river was pouring from her back. By then the backup had arrived, and they took Jacqueline into custody. Blood covered Martha with a perfectly round hole in her chest. He could not find a pulse. He called for an ambulance and waited powerlessly for them to arrive.

The EMTs checked Martha, looked up and said, "She is alive."

They rushed Martha to the hospital. She went into surgery immediately. Ken waited outside with Ruth and Mary, pacing the floor, and praying.

Two hours later, the surgeon came in to talk to the family, "She's a lucky girl. The bullet missed anything vital. It passed just an inch from her heart. She's going to be sore, but my prognosis is she will fully recover."

Ken sat by her bedside, holding her hand, waiting, and praying. He was struggling to keep his eyes open, and as he drifted off to sleep, her hand stirred. He looked up to see her sparkling green eyes opening.

"How are you feeling?" Ken asked.

"Sore. What happened?"

"You took a bullet to the chest you're lucky to be alive."

"What about Jacqueline, how is she?"

"She's alive but just keeps babbling about family being the most important thing."

"And her mom and dad?"

Ken slowly shook his head, "They picked them up at the airport in Columbus coming in from Washington DC."

"At least they will not hurt the girls anymore."

"The crime scene team is taking apart the Phillips' house right now. They have already found several of Jacqueline's journals, and she documented every time her father was with her. She was also with other Senators and Congress men. Both Rick and Elizabeth used her as a honey pot trap. It's going to be really hard for them to talk their way out of this. The

Chief is getting pressure from Washington to hush this thing up. She has been told if she speaks out, she was finished."

"Finished?"

"She wants to speak out, but powerful people are lining up against her."

Martha winced with the pain, "But two meaningless deaths to cover up this secret."

"Make that four, according to her journal, her father had hired Harvey Franks, but when he failed, he sent Jacqueline to eliminate him."

"He sent Jacqueline?"

"He would wind her up emotionally and then send her out to do his dirty work. If you had read a few pages before the murder of your father, you would've found out that her father was the one behind it all."

"So, he was using her like a weapon."

"Yes, he sent her to kill your father, Detective Malroy, Billy, and Harvey Franks."

"Billy?"

"Billy."

"Poor girl, I feel sorry for her."

"Don't feel too sorry, she almost killed you to. In fact, she would've, if we hadn't shown up."

"This needs reporting. Hand me my phone."

She looked up Sherry Porters number. She dialed.

"Sherry, this is Martha Thomas. Have I got a story for you."

"That should do it."

"Thank you for your good timing. Now I think I'm going to get a little sleep."

As her eyes went closed, she said, "You know I said it wasn't time for a relationship, now I think it's time."

As she slipped into sleep she said, "Maybe I'll see you at church."